DEDICATION

I would like to dedicate this book to the great people and places of Cornwall - I have grown to love and cherish you so much. To my sister Catherine for her inspiration and encouragement. To my group of proofreaders and supporters. To everyone affected by an alcoholic parent. Stay strong. Time heals.

PROLOGUE

Location: Trellinick, North Cornwall, 2022

Supper Club had long been the highlight of our week. Although Hetty was hosting this particular evening, I couldn't help interfering. I would have preferred to call it helping, but no, she insisted it was interference.

The truth was, I couldn't stand by while carrots, onions, and potatoes were chopped into wildly irregular shapes. The preparation was beginning to resemble animal feed more than a gourmet dinner.

When I finally stepped in, Hetty raised her eyes at Albert, thinking, or at least hoping, I hadn't noticed. He raised his glass in silent solidarity, both of them grinning like naughty children. The pair of them were incorrigible when wine was involved.

I took the knife and began slicing with precision, salvaging the chaos Hetty had left behind.

Vegetable massacre aside, the evening was, as always, filled with laughter, food (beautifully finished, if I may say so) and a few more glasses of wine than anticipated. Hetty was her usual mischievous self; Albert, quietly dignified, drank in our antics as well as the pinot grigio.

I loved what we had here at Beachcombers. A simple life, yes. But one rich in friendship, not wealth. The joy we found came not from possessions, but from each other.

After dinner, we sat with glasses of port, listening to the wind roll across the exposed bay. Then Hetty mentioned William.

As always, my heart faltered. My hand instinctively

Only the Lonely

Gráinne McGovern-Scott

ISBN: 979-828-9314-88-8

moved to my mouth to contain the gasp.

Hetty knew my story better than anyone. She understood the weight of William's absence. She only mentioned him now as part of a conversation about our children's birth years, never to exclude him, never to pretend he hadn't existed. We all knew he had. And as far as we knew, he still did. The pain came from not knowing where.

We ended the night with warm hugs and well, worn jokes before each retreating to our perfectly kept mobile homes. None of us had the faintest idea of the events that would begin to unfold just hours later.

PART ONE

Discovery

CHAPTER ONE
Marjorie

I used to tell people Audrey Hepburn was my cousin. Not seriously of course, just as a child. A little lie I told so often I almost believed it.

We shared a surname and that felt like fate. I was just one Christian name away. Marjorie May Hepburn. Not quite as elegant, not quite as famous but close enough that I imagined we were connected by something more than coincidence.

I knew her films by heart, Roman Holiday, Sabrina, Breakfast at Tiffany's. I practised her expressions in the mirror, the wide eyes, the tilted chin. I even tried to copy the way she held a teacup, as if it were the most delicate thing in the world.

Mum said I was being silly. That no one in our family had ever been glamorous, and we ought to be proud of that. She said people like Audrey belonged to another world. "Pretty nonsense," she called it.

I never saw it that way.

I didn't want the fame; I wanted the stillness. The way Audrey looked like she knew something the rest of us didn't. The way she carried sadness like silk, quiet, uncreased.

I never told anyone about that. Except Hetty. She laughed, but gently. Said it made sense, really I was always trying to straighten the world out like a hemline.

Now, I live in a mobile home park in North Cornwall. No pearls. No Givenchy. Just a good kettle, a decent view of the dunes, and Hetty across the way in a dressing gown that hasn't seen a hanger since 2004. We both also had the indomitable Albert, sweet, generous, and incredibly tolerant. A friend if every sense of the word.

This place may not be glamorous, but it's mine. When the wind's up and the gulls are soaring across laden skies, I still allow myself to imagine Audrey would have liked it here too.

The reality of my world now however, revolves around a routine that blankets me in comfort. I wake around seven. After finishing my lemon tea, I shower, dress and armed with a toasted teacake and a flask of English breakfast tea, take the short walk down to my favourite bench just above the dunes of Trellinick Bay.

Rain, wind, or shine, this is how I choose to welcome the day.

I seldom see anyone. Occasionally, a dog walker or beachcomber might cross my path scavenging for driftwood or whatever treasures the night tide has left behind. But I don't seek conversation not at that hour. A polite nod or wave is more than enough. This is my time.

The habit began when I moved to Beachcombers ten years ago. Our little mobile home park, perched here on the north Cornish coast, comprises twelve homes with grey slate pitched roofs, all with views most people only dream of. The beach, the dunes, the bench, I've known them all my whole life. For sixty-eight years they've been my sanctuary. I've laughed here, cried here, loved and lost here.

This morning, the wind, though not cold, raced in hard across the bay, churning the sea into a wild mess of foam and greys. Seaweed danced erratically in the surf, while gulls hovered and veered like puppets on broken strings. Larger waves hurled themselves at the rocks to the left of the bay with theatrical force.

I was grateful for the air. A little too much pinot grigio at Hetty's supper club had left me woolly-headed. I'd hoped the salt spray might sort me out. It usually did.

I settled on my bench, turned on the radio set to low volume just enough to keep me company. Farming Today was halfway through an interview about scallop beds when I noticed something down by the grasses near the strandline.

Something dark. Unfamiliar.

It could have been a rucksack. Or a bin bag. Or just the way the sand had shifted overnight. I squinted but didn't move. It was just off to my right, but frankly, I wasn't in the mood for beachcombing.

Probably just a forgotten wetsuit.

I finished my tea and looked away.

CHAPTER TWO
Hetty

Beachcombers is my haven. A horseshoe of twelve homes with neat gardens and a central, ivy, covered pergola where we sit and chat and in the summer, sip wine until the midges chase us indoors.

As people no longer tethered to young children or full-time jobs, our wealth comes from each other, not from generously filled bank accounts. That suits us just fine.

I came here ten years ago with my lifelong friend, Marjorie Hepburn. We were both bruised and disillusioned by what life had thrown at us, and Beachcombers offered the blank page we needed. Joining us was the indomitable Albert. The third point on a triangular friendship unbroken by lifes events.

For me, it was a chance to recover from the slow heartbreak of watching my husband dissolve into alcoholism.

I stayed with Edwin far longer than I should have, through failed interventions, through the shouting, the smashed glasses, the promises that shattered as soon as they were made. I stayed until there was nothing left to save, and then, finally, he left me before I could leave him. He pressed the self-destruct button himself.

He had been my world. He and our three children were everything. Edwin was my first and only love, and I gave my life to him. Our story began here in Trellinick, how strange and sad that it wouldn't end here too.

Running alongside that love story was Marjorie.

We met at the village primary school, innocent four-year olds, blissfully unaware that no amount of schooling could prepare us for what life had in store. That we're still best friends now, neighbours, no less, says everything about what we've weathered. Fate anchored us here for different reasons, but somehow our ships landed side by side.

It's hard to explain what makes our friendship work so well. We're quite different women. I'm the whirlwind to her calm, I speak my mind, sometimes when I shouldn't, while she takes her time, measures her words, and sees the world with more grace than most.

And yet we never fall out. Never walk away. We are, to each other, essential.

As children, we played endlessly. As teenagers, we discovered boys, booze, and the sharp edges of heartbreak. But as adults, when life truly knocked us down, our bond became something more than friendship.

It became survival.

Marjorie stood by me through so many awful nights with Edwin. She held my hand when I couldn't explain the bruises. She watched my children when I couldn't face them myself. And never, not once, did she judge me for staying.

She knew why I did. She knew I loved him. I needed to believe he could change.

It was naïve, but it was love.

Nowadays, life is simpler. I'm sixty-eight, still healthy, still busy, but I enjoy the quiet. I adore it when my children visit with the grandchildren. But I also adore it when they leave, when I can reclaim my cushions, put the tippy cups away, and light a candle without fear of anyone setting fire to it.

I have Marjorie. I have Albert.

And I have peace.

CHAPTER THREE
Albert

I never imagined I'd live in a mobile home park, let alone enjoy it. And yet here I am, ten years in, part of an unlikely little community on the Cornish coast, and happier than I have any right to be.

Beachcombers drew me in gently. I'd come down for a long weekend at the invitation of some university friends and left with a deposit paid and a vision of retirement I'd never planned.

At first, I wasn't sure I'd stay. I thought I might use it as a base for a year or two, while I sorted through the mess Kathleen left behind. But then I met Hetty and Marjorie, and the idea of "leaving" slowly lost all meaning.

They welcomed me like an old friend. Marjorie, with her quiet dignity and eyes that always seem to measure kindness. Hetty, loud and laughable and full of opinions she rarely filters. Together, they made space for me, not out of pity, but in the way of people who have learned how to carry pain and still make room at the table.

Colleagues, family, especially my daughter, Emily, all questioned my decision to stay here. Why, after forty years as a GP with a handsome pension and an inheritance most people would envy, would I choose to live in a mobile home on the Cornish coast?

The answer was simple. Wealth, to me, wasn't measured in numbers. It's something deeper; a life grounded in simplicity, truth, and friendship.

Our Supper Club became an institution. We rotate weekly. The rules are simple: home-cooked meals, no politics, and always pudding. I'm no chef, but I've mastered a few casseroles, and discovered, to my great surprise, that I enjoy baking.

Emily finds this hilarious. Kathleen would have too; I spent most of our marriage pretending I didn't know what a sieve was.

Kathleen. I still wear my ring. Still speak to her sometimes, though I wouldn't admit it to the others. It's not madness, it's habit. Decades of conversation don't just stop because someone leaves.

She was my compass. And when we ended... the map became harder to read.

Emily did her best in those early days. She came down from London most weekends, checking I was eating, that I hadn't joined a wine club by accident or let the potted plants wither in protest. Eventually she eased off. I began to find my own rhythm again, slowly, stubbornly. And of course I had my two Albert-sitters, Hetty next to me, Marjorie across the way.

It was Hetty who really pulled me back into life. She has a way of making you laugh even when you don't want to. I once told her that grief, or whatever you'd call this quiet absence, had made me hollow. She said, "Good. Now there's space to put things in."

I don't know if she meant it to be profound, but it was.

Now, when I walk across the green in the mornings and wave at Marjorie tending her window boxes or see Hetty wrestling with her compost bin or chasing after her grandson, I feel something close to peace. Not the absence of pain, but the presence of something healing.

It's a curious thing, starting over at seventy.

But here I am.

Still learning.

Still trying.

Still here.

CHAPTER FOUR
Marjorie

The wind, calmer than yesterday, still sent swirls of sand skimming across the beach. As always, it was empty but for gulls, lunging and diving playfully against the breeze.

I packed my breakfast picnic as usual and made my way to the bench above the dunes.

But I couldn't sit.

Something tugged at me.

The dark shape I'd seen the day before was still there, half-concealed by tufts of marram grass near the strandline. Most things disappear overnight on this beach: bits of netting, shoes, the odd crisp packet. But this hadn't moved. Curiosity got the better of me.

I set my cup down, walked the few steps across the damp sand. The closer I got, the more certain I became, it wasn't rubbish. It was bag.

A holdall. Black. Zipped. Worn but intact. A faded Nike logo. A leather name tag flapped furiously in the wind, blank. No name. No hint of ownership. The clear plastic window cracked - whatever had once been in there by way of identification, now lost no doubt to the wind.

I knelt beside it and pushed it with my hands. It didn't move easily. It wasn't clothing. Not a discarded towel or lunchbox. I looked around. The beach was still empty, as was the distant car park. No cars. No camper vans.

The wind had taken hold of my hood making it flap back and forth like a windsock. The fine grains of sand like stinging nettles against my face forced me to squint and cover my eyes with my arm.

I unzipped it just a few inches, enough to allow me to see what was inside.

Bundles.

Cling-wrapped. Tightly stacked. Unmistakable.

Cash.

Stunned I zipped it shut, stood so fast I stumbled backwards into the dunes. I slowly got to my knees and scanned the dunes. Still no one. Just gulls and waves and the sound of blood rushing in my ears.

I clambered up and stood there for a full minute, willing my brain to make sense of it. My heart was working overtime as I tried to tell myself to calm down.

And then I did what I never imagined I would do.

I picked it up and walked home.

Not in a rush. Not running. Just walking, like someone who'd collected a loaf of bread and was heading back before the butter melted. I thought if I acted normal, I might feel normal.

I didn't.

By the time I reached Beachcombers, my hands were damp on the holdall straps and my breath had shortened into sharp little gasps. I unlocked the door, stepped inside, and locked it again. Twice. Deadlocked.

The bag thumped onto the rug like a dead animal.

I turned the radio off. Then back on. Then off again.

What was I doing?

I carried the bag into the bedroom and shoved it under the bed, without looking inside again. Wrapped it in a towel. Then, unsure that was enough, I added my *'yet to be used'* sleeping bag. It was the first time it had ever felt remotely useful.

I washed my hands. Boiled the kettle. Stared at the teapot as it filled. Forgot the teabags.

I tried to sit and couldn't. My limbs twitched with adrenaline. My mind reeled through worst-case scenarios: CCTV. Helicopters. Drug dealers realising their drop had gone missing and tracing it to an older lady with a flask and a fondness for benches.

Only the Lonely

What had I done?

Why did I bring it here?

I stood in the kitchen for fifteen minutes before I finally reached for my phone and typed one sentence to Hetty:

> *Come over. Urgently. Bring your calmest self. Make sure you're dressed. No pyjamas in public.*

I might have been in a panic, but I had standards that were sometimes lost on Hetty.

I stood at my window discreetly and watched her locking her home and walk across the green.

I met her at the door. "Did anybody follow you over here, Hetty?"

She gave me a look. "You literally just watched me walk over, Miss Marple. Who would have followed me, and why? Did you put something stronger in your flask this morning?"

"Don't be daft. Come in. Now pull the curtains, I don't want anyone peering through the windows. I'll get what I found. It's under the bed."

"What the hell, Marjorie? Have you started dealing drugs or something? What did you find on that beach that's got you acting like this? This is Trellinick, not the Bronx. If this is a shell with the face of Jesus on it, I will not be impressed."

I bounced on the spot like a child needing the loo. "No, it's not a shell. Not even a *bleedin'* shell. You'd do well to have a bit of Jesus shell art in your life, by the way. Just sit, no, not there, there. The sofa. I'll be back in a minute."

Hetty sighed but obeyed. She drew the drapes shut, flicked on the lights, and perched on the designated seat with exaggerated impatience.

I knelt, reached under the bed, and dragged out the bag. Still wrapped in towels and the sleeping bag, a raffle prize from four years ago. (Wild horses couldn't drag me into a tent, let alone a sleeping bag.) I returned the towels to the bathroom and shoved the sleeping bag back into its cover.

The bag still felt heavy. As heavy as it had before. I wasn't sure if that wasn't just the weight of the guilt I felt bringing this illegitimate haul back to my perfectly legitimate home.

I carried it to the lounge, where Hetty was flicking through my Homes & Gardens magazine with a tad too much enthusiasm.

"You've not crumpled that, have you? Hetty, you are so heavy-handed. I don't like my pages crumpled up."

"Chill out. I was just flicking through it while you retrieved the Elgin Marbles."

"Well, it's not quite the Elgin Marbles. Now, Hetty," I said, placing the bag on the floor, "what I'm about to show you is confidential. I haven't looked again since I returned to my property. I zipped it back up and called you."

Hetty laughed. "Bloody hell, Marjorie. '*Returned to your property*'? I'm not the police. It's probably just clothes. Did you find it on the beach? Open it and let's see."

"Yes, I found it on the beach. And no, it's not clothes. It's this."

I laid a bath towel across the carpet (just in case there was sand), set the bag on top, and slowly unzipped it.

Out tumbled bundles of cash. Crisp. Clingfilm wrapped. Tightly packed.

We stared at the pile in stunned silence.

Hetty slapped her hands to her cheeks. "Oh my goodness, Marjorie! What the hell have you found?"

I knelt closer. Most of the weight, it turned out, came from two large rocks, clearly added to help conceal it in the dunes.

"How much do you think is here?"

"I honestly don't know." I felt my stomach twist. "Hetty, what have I done bringing this here? Am I part of something criminal now? What if they come looking for it? I should've left it. Should I take it back?"

"Calm down. Nobody goes to that beach at this time of day, except you. Truth be told, nobody really goes to that beach other than us, and a few village dog walkers. If the police come knocking, you just hand it over. Say you were going to take it in but hadn't got round to it yet. Where was it? Surely not on your bench?"

I pushed my back against the sofa. "No not on my bench, just off to the right of it though. I honestly wish it was a shell with Jesus on it now."

Hetty looked at me like I'd gone mad, "Marjorie, this is way better than any holy shell. Think of all the things you could do with this money?"

We sat in silence. Then giggled. Then sat in silence again.

We were totally out of our depth.

We both knew what we had to do.

Albert.

CHAPTER FIVE
Hetty

Marjorie Hepburn what have you done? Her decision to carry that bag of cash back to her house was the wildest thing she's ever done in her life. In any of our lives.

When we were teenagers, she was the sensible one, home by curfew, sober and tidy. I, on the other hand, lived more on the edge. I liked to push the boundaries. Kiss the boys and make them cry. Let's just say I cast my net wide.

Marjorie had Michael. They were deeply in love, such as we understood love back then.

I remember the sadness in her when he told her he was leaving Trellinick. A pain I honestly believe he shared to be fair to him. His father had found him a job as a trainee accountant in Exeter, and he was to leave within the month. I honestly thought they'd marry one day, but he'd been clear:

"Forget about me, Marjorie. I've loved you more than you'll ever know, but dad has plans for me beyond Trellinick, and I have to go. I see no life for us outside of what we shared here."

Little did he know, little did she know, he had already given her the most perfect little life before he left. The surprise none of us saw coming.

Back in her living room, we were motionless knelt on her living room floor. I broke the silence and said we should give it a week.

Seven days to see if anyone came looking for the bag. Seven days to decide if this was a gift, a curse, or something far more complicated.

It had been two hours.

And now I was staring at the contents of a bag that looked like something from a heist film in Marjorie's sitting room.

"Bloody hell." I whispered, hands still pressed to my face.

Wrong was one word for it. Illegal was another. Life-changing, there was that too.

We stared for a moment longer, then she moved, zipping the bag closed, lifting it with surprising steadiness, and disappearing down the hallway. I heard the bedroom door open. The flapping of towels. Then silence. The two rocks that had weighed it down in the dunes sat on her rug like two breasts devoid of bra.

I picked them up and pushed them up my jumper.

When she returned, she looked pale. "Hetty!"

"Reckon I could get a boob job with that money Marj. Dya think it would suit me?"

"Honestly, put them down before one of them falls on your toes and we have that to explain in A&E. We need to tell Albert."

"Thank God," I said. "I was hoping you'd say that."

Albert arrived within the hour, scarf slightly askew, bag in hand.

"I assumed it was either a crime or a crisis," he said. "So, I brought biscuits."

Marjorie led us to the kitchen. The kettle was already boiling, that was her way. Crisis, calm, or company, she boiled water.

I opened the wine instead. This meeting didn't call for tea.

Once we were settled, she told him everything, from the bench to the beach, the bag, the panic. She spoke slowly, carefully, as if saying it aloud might make it sound more sensible.

Albert sat motionless, hands clasped, lips tight, eyes focused.

He didn't interrupt, save for pushing his glasses up the bridge of his nose or sipping his wine, he'd passed on the tea, too.

When she finished, he said simply, "Well. That is… unexpected."

We waited.

"I think you did the right thing, not opening it wide on the beach. And the right thing in not telling anyone else. I'm glad you called me."

"You're not going to tell us to call the police?" Marjorie asked.

He paused. "I'm going to suggest we think very, very carefully. This wasn't lost by accident. It was placed, hidden deliberately. With rocks to weigh it down. Close to your bench you said Marjorie but not right next to it. Not so close to the bench that you could imagine someone was sat on it, put the bag down next to them and then walked away accidently leaving it behind. That makes it suspicious. In my humble opinion, this bag wasn't lost, it was left. The question is for whom?"

"Could it be criminal?" I asked.

"Potentially," he said. "Or something else entirely. But either way, it carries risk."

We all fell silent. The clock ticked. Somewhere outside, the wind shifted, rattling the window vents with a soft whistle.

I topped up our glasses. "So, what do we do?"

Albert looked at each of us in turn.

"For now, we wait. No spending. No moving it again. Just... wait. Seven days, you said?"

I nodded.

"Then let's stick to that. And in the meantime, let's not do anything foolish."

Marjorie's shoulders dropped an inch. Not relief, exactly, but a small comfort. She wasn't alone in the madness anymore.

That night we were quieter than usual. Three old friends, with a secret bigger than any of us had ever imagined.

Supper was simple. Cheese, ham, crackers, and Marjorie's coffee and walnut cake.

I wasn't sure if the feeling in my chest was excitement

or dread. Maybe both.
Either way, our peace had been disturbed.
And for once, it felt good.

CHAPTER SIX
Albert

Marjorie looked lighter, but not in the joyful sense. More like someone bracing herself for the next part of something she didn't choose. And Hetty had that spark in her eyes again, the one she gets during Monday quiz nights when she thinks she's on an unbeatable team.

They'd done something. That much was obvious.

When I stepped into Marjorie's home, she was already in the kitchen, fussing with the kettle. I clocked the bag immediately - by the armchair, tucked into the shadow, as if a floral throw might somehow disguise it. But there it was, quiet, hulking, and impossible to ignore.

Hetty was pointing to it and mouthing its contents to me in an exaggerated charade I had no understanding of. I got 'bag' and 'beach' but before I could decipher anymore Marjorie came into the living room.

She poured tea with trembling hands. Two china cups on matching saucers for us, a generous glass of wine for Hetty, who perched at the table like a gossip columnist waiting for the scoop.

After a few sips, Marjorie told me everything. No ceremony, no buildup, just facts. Where she found it. What she saw. What she felt. Then the panic. Then the call.

I listened. I didn't interrupt, though every part of me wanted to. But there's a time for questions, and a time for quiet.

When she finished, I looked at the bag. Still zipped, thankfully.

"I think," I said, "we need to be extremely careful."

They both nodded.

"I'm not suggesting we turn it over, not yet, not without understanding what we're dealing with. But if this is what it looks like, it's not just a windfall. It's someone's loss. Possibly someone dangerous. Possibly someone who'll come looking."

He paused. Took off his glasses and rubbed his eyes before continuing.

"It's puzzling though. How does one forget a bag filled with cash? You said it had been there the day before Marjorie, and you're quite sure it was the same bag?"

"Oh yes I'm quite sure. I'm just cross I didn't look yesterday."

"No actually that's good. If it had been forgotten, surely that someone would have realised and returned to collect it yesterday. Equally if it was meant for collection in some sort of illegal enterprise, why leave it over twenty-four hours and why have the collection point next to an often-frequented bench on a public beach?"

Marjorie paled. Hetty, unusually, didn't speak. They just looked at one another, then back to me.

"I'll make some discreet enquiries. Hypothetical ones. I have a solicitor friend from my university days. We have enough on each other for me to know she won't ask too many questions. I'll say I'm researching a writing project. Fiction obviously."

Hetty raised an eyebrow. "You're writing a novel now?"

"If it keeps Marjorie out of jail, I'll write a bloody trilogy."

That got a laugh. A real one, from both of them. Tense, but there.

I didn't stay long. I left them with the mystery haul and told them I'd be in touch once I knew anything useful. As I stepped out into the breeze, it tugged at my scarf, and for a moment, I felt the familiar ache of uncertainty. The kind you get when you know you've crossed into new territory.

I'd been a doctor long enough to know that people often do the wrong thing for the right reasons, or vice versa.

The trick was knowing which was which. And when.

Back home, I sat in the quiet, my mind drifting to Kathleen the embodiment of that conundrum.

Somehow, and rather sadly, the irony wasn't lost on me that she would have understood the need for secrecy.

It was secrecy, in the end, that undid us.

I picked up the phone and called Ruth, the one friend I could trust with odd questions.

"I'm doing some research," I said. "Fictional. About a character who finds a bag of money on a beach."

There was a pause.

"You're not going to like this," she said. "There are all sorts of laws, and finders keepers isn't one of them."

"Say hypothetically, for the sake of my story, it was abandoned. Left, rather than lost. Weighted down to stay hidden. Loser's weepers doesn't apply then, because it wasn't lost it was deliberately left and not by accident."

"That's the trick. Proving it was. Tell your fictional character to be very careful. Even good deeds can land people in hot water."

I thanked her, made a few notes I knew I'd never show anyone. Then in need of sugary comfort, I snapped a rather large piece of chocolate from a bar that had been lingering in my fridge. I don't often indulge in sweet treats but occasionally, when the situation demanded it, I allowed myself to. This was just such an occasion.

The storm hadn't arrived yet.

But I had a feeling it would.

CHAPTER SEVEN
Hetty

What a morning Marjorie.

A bag full of cash, who else but her could stumble across something so utterly insane and still manage to fold it into her daily routine like it was a new brand of biscuits? That said, there was no question it had created a sense of unease for us all.

After I left her that morning, I couldn't stop thinking about the look on her face. Calm on the outside, but inside, I knew she was pacing. Weighing the morality of it all like a courtroom judge. Tea in one hand, guilt in the other.

I texted her later. Told her to come over for lunch if she was spiralling. I didn't want her alone with all that silence.

She's had enough of that for one lifetime.

I keep thinking, if anyone deserved a bit of unexpected fortune, it's Marjorie Hepburn. Her life's been a mosaic of loss, silence, and other people making decisions on her behalf. Maybe, just maybe, this was the universe finally tipping something in her favour.

Finding the three of us, her, Albert, and me, wasn't luck. It was necessity. We're all a little bit broken, but our edges fit together. Between us, the sting of loneliness softens. Most days, anyway.

Of course, we all have our ghosts.

Mine wore Edwin's face.

The biggest contradiction I've ever known. Charming, magnetic, and utterly unreliable. Until he took a drink. I gave him chance after chance, each one thinner than the last. Told him, "If you do it again, I'm gone." But he knew. He always knew. Knew I had nowhere to go. Knew I loved him too much to leave, even when he shattered everything.

There weren't shelters back then. No helplines. Just women like me, learning how to shrink ourselves.

Sometimes I wonder if he ever really tried to change, or if he was just playing the part. He'd promise, of course. Apologise with flowers. Dote on the children like he was trying out for Father of the Year, then drink it all into ruins again.

The night that broke me was Aladdin.

All three of our children were in the school play. Sebastian, our eldest, was cast as the lead. He was so proud. Practised his lines until he whispered them in his sleep. Of all my children, Sebastian was the most sensitive. A shy, deeply thoughtful boy. When he was chosen as the lead, he cried telling me. He simply so proud.

Edwin swore he'd come. Promised he'd stay sober.

He didn't.

I sat in that school hall alone. Clapped until my hands stung. And all the while, I scanned the crowd, praying Edwin would appear like a last-minute miracle.

He never did.

After the show, my sweet boy looked down from the stage and mouthed, '*Where's dad?*'

My heart broke. Not just for the absence, but for the recognition in Sebastians face. The quiet disappointment of a child already used to being let down.

Later, I found out Edwin was in a cell. Another brawl. Another drunken night. Another excuse. I remember watching him step out of that police car two days later, and all I could feel was dread, disgust and disappointment. Not because he was home, but because he hadn't died. On the morning of the second day of his absence, I'd allowed myself to believe he wasn't coming back.

I wanted him gone. Really gone.

I've never said that out loud. Not even to Marjorie.

But that night, standing on the porch, watching him walk up the drive, I wished with every fibre of my body that he'd stayed wherever he'd been. That would have meant we could finally breathe and sleep safe in our beds at night.

Goodness, what kind of person thinks that?

I guess the kind who'd simply had enough.

The kind who was struggling to survive

I remember Sebastian telling me one evening that he often heard us fighting. He said the noise of the shouting and crying was hard to hear but it was the silence that came after that frightened him more. He'd lie there worrying he'd killed me, or I'd killed Edwin.

That poor child. He'd crawl into Chloe's bed, and they'd comfort each other till the morning which would reveal my fresh bruises, the broken furniture, the blooded walls.

Maybe that's why the bag doesn't scare me like it scares Marjorie. I've spent a lifetime fighting bigger dilemma's than a mysterious bag of money hidden in the dunes.

Yet I know that's unfair.

I know she knows what it feels like to be powerless. To have your choices taken until you forget you ever had them. I know she is a moral lady. Someone for whom doing anything illegal would give her sleepless nights.

So yes, I want her to keep it.

Not to spend on nonsense. Not to hoard. But to use.

To take back her story.

She's been stuck on that bench with grief like a shadow for too long. This money, whatever it is, wherever it came from, it's a key. And I'll be damned if I let her lock the door again.

CHAPTER EIGHT
Marjorie

I hadn't stopped thinking about it. Not for a moment.

The bag sat under the bed like a secret I'd willingly adopted but didn't know how to raise. It breathed in the quiet. It shifted my thoughts. It made everything else, meals, television, crosswords, feel frivolous and faintly ridiculous.

Albert had said we'd wait. A week. Seven days to see if anyone came looking, if anything was mentioned in the news, if the universe sent a signal.

It had been three.

I told myself I was being patient. That I was simply watching, not worrying. But the truth was, I hadn't slept properly. I'd stared out the front window so often that the condensation formed in familiar shapes. I jumped whenever the post came. I maintained my morning ritual. The last three days Hetty and Albert had come too, "just in case" they said.

Just in case what? I dreaded to think. Hetty had come armed with a rape whistle from a Police Force talk she'd been to with her daughter on 'female safety.' What possible use that would be on an empty beach only Hetty knew. Much as I appreciated their presence there, they were actually making me more nervous, so I politely suggested that I go alone from now on. They both looked relieved, though Hetty insisted I take her whistle with me. So, it's there, packed in my morning beach bag. I'm certainly not wearing it like a medal. Unlike Hetty.

By the fourth day, something shifted. Not outside, but in me.

I thought about the money constantly. The fear of someone coming to look for it on the one hand, and on the other, the realisation that it had been four days, and we were now closer to day seven. Nobody had come. No strangers lurking near the park. No cars parked where there shouldn't be. No strangers skulking on the beach. Could I possibly be in the clear?

I told Hetty the next morning, not as a confession, but to have her reassure me that she was beginning to think the same way.

"I haven't done anything," I said. "But are we getting close?"

Hetty raised one eyebrow, then poured me tea like I'd just told her I was thinking of getting a tattoo. A prospect I can assure you has never crossed my mind. Hetty, on the other hand, now sported three tattoos, an angel on her shoulder, a heart containing her grandchildren's names on her wrist, and a down arrow somewhere private. I'm assuming that's for her amusement only these days, though this is Hetty, so who knows.

"Well," she said, "you've got restraint, Marjorie. If it were me, I'd have been digging into that cash every day for a little something or other. I've always wanted my teeth whitened."

"Hetty, no. Your teeth are perfectly fine. Anyway, I couldn't," I whispered. "Not yet. Albert said,"

"I know what Albert said," she interrupted gently. "And he's right. But I'd love to see you live a bit for once, Marjorie. Spoil yourself."

I didn't answer directly, but we grinned conspiratorially at each other.

Later, we sat on the bench and watched the sea gnaw at the shore. The same tide, the same gulls, the same old stretch of sky. The same rape alarm.

I let the silence carry what I wasn't sure I was ready to. My mind drifted to William. As ever, Hetty recognised to whom my mind had wondered and put her head on my shoulder and took my hand. "We've got this Marjorie, you're not alone. We're in this life together. Always."

CHAPTER NINE
Albert

It was Hetty who brought it up, casually, over a bacon sandwich in my kitchen, as if we were discussing the weather.

"You know who she's thinking about again, don't you?" she said, not looking at me.

I didn't have to ask. "William."

She nodded.

"She's trying not to. But she is."

I passed her the ketchup. We can really pour it on when Marjorie isn't with us. "It's understandable."

Hetty sighed. "I know you might not fully appreciate what that beach represents to us. To Marjorie in particular. She sat on that bench, on that beach, the night Michael told her he was leaving her. She was heartbroken. We both were. It was such a shock."

She pushed the swell of emotion down with a large gulp of tea.

"That money's unsettled us all. But why? I'm sorry to get so upset, I just hate the injustice of it all. We should all be jumping through hoops, but we're not. I wonder if she shouldn't just hand it over. But then I think no, why the hell should she?"

I let her speak. Sometimes people don't want advice, just air.

"I've known Marjorie since we were four," she said. "The kindest, most incredible friend, yet dealt the harshest, cruellest hand by her own so-called mother. I think she feels so guilty about William. He permeates every inch of her brain. Do you think she regrets not trying harder to find him?"

"I think she regrets not being allowed to," I said.

Hetty didn't reply to that, but her eyes softened.

"I wish we'd known you back then. You would have known where we stood, how to get William back. Even if it took years, you'd have known. We didn't have the knowhow. All we had was each other and the pain of it all."

"It's never too late to right a wrong you know Hetty. Maybe some good could come of this money. I think you both know by the way, that I am also fallible and quite capable of getting things wrong. I don't see my wife here next to me."

She sighed deeply and squeezed my hand.

"Oh Albert. What are we like, the three of us. Living our very own versions of The Jeremy Kyle Show."

"Who's Jeremy Kyle?"

Hetty smiled as she gathered our breakfast plates and stacked them by the sink, "Nobody. Don't worry. He wouldn't be your cup of tea."

We stayed at the table a while, me nursing the pen that was meant to be completing The Times crossword. Hetty clicking on her phone sending photographs of her grandchildren to what were presumably happy recipients.

She put the phone down, and with her fist propped under her chin asked,

"Do you still love Kathleen, Albert? I mean, can't you see a way past what happened?"

I was somewhat surprised by Hetty's directness - though frankly after ten years of knowing her, I shouldn't have been. Neither she nor Marjorie had ever questioned me about her. Not in quite so pointed a way. They knew who she was, or at least who she had been to me. They knew she had hurt me terribly, but not the details.

Kathleen had turned what our entire relationship had been based on into a lie. I simply couldn't get beyond that.

We'd stopped living together a year before I came to

Beachcombers. We never divorced. Never fought. Just... stepped away. She called sometimes. We still spoke about Emily, birthdays, logistics, weather.

But the centre had gone.

Some truths, once spoken, make the rest of your life feel quieter by comparison.

"I will always love her Hetty. I love what we had. I love who she was to me and Emily. Can I see past what happened? Maybe, one day. Maybe I'm being a stubborn old fool not letting her back in. Maybe I'm still punishing her for what she did to me. Who knows. Maybe I'm just scared of making that first move."

"You literally just said, 'it never too late to right a wrong, Albert.' Don't let your own advice fall on deaf ears. If you're just being stubborn, then give that clever head of yours a wobble and sort this out. Life's too short surely you can see that."

I gave her a little nudge, "Well you know what they say old girl, the plumbers tap is always leaking. Maybe I'm just not ready or brave enough to pick up the wrench yet and fix it."

She smiled playfully at me as she stretched her arms out and called time on our breakfast meeting. She pecked my cheek as she always did, and as she reached the door she turned,

"Well Albie old boy, if you don't pick that wrench up soon, someone else might and we don't want any old tradesman at that sink do we?." Then she winked at me and left.

That thought had entered my mind of course. It had been over ten years since our separation and whilst there hadn't appeared to a new love interest in Kathleen's life, I couldn't guarantee there never would be. She was still as stunning as she always had been.

I loaded the dishwasher, wiped the surfaces, Marjorie would be proud, and attempted the crossword for the second time. Still unsuccessfully.

My thoughts had turned back to Majorie and what Hetty had said about the beach, Michael leaving and William's removal. I knew what Hetty was hinting at. Perhaps I could have done more.

I didn't search adoption records or message boards the way I knew I could. I didn't ask medical colleagues to check databases or GP files. Not because I didn't care, but because I did. Because I knew that if he ever returned, it should be for her. But there was a selfish reason too.

I couldn't risk knowing something about William's fate that I wasn't then prepared to share with his mother. That would simply make me another person hiding secrets from her about her son. I simply couldn't do that.

I folded the newspaper away. The crossword could wait.

CHAPTER TEN
Hetty

I couldn't help but be amused watching Albert grapple with The Times crossword. He has this habit of pushing his glasses to the tip of his nose and gazing up at the heavens, as though divine intervention might deliver the answer. There was plenty of heaven-gazing going on that morning.

To be fair, I'd interrupted him with deeply personal questions, which can't have helped his concentration. Probably unfair of me, really. Albert and an unfinished crossword are not a happy combination, and I didn't want to be the one responsible for throwing him off.

I left him intending to walk the short path home, but instead my feet carried me through Beachcombers and onto the beach. I felt a flicker of guilt about asking Albert about Kathleen. He'd answered willingly enough, but it's rare for him to open up like that. I just wish he'd take the brave step and tell her how he feels. Our conversation only strengthened that hope.

I sat on Marjorie's bench. It's easy to see why she loves it, not just for the view or the memories, but the quiet steadiness of it. I glanced across at the dune where she'd found the bag. The marram grasses, once flattened by its weight, were swaying gently again, as though untouched by their role in our drama. The three of us though, we hadn't bounced back nearly as well. We were still stuck somewhere between fear, excitement, and confusion.

If the grasses could recover, surely we could too.

When we were teenagers, Marjorie, Michael, Edwin and I would all sit on this bench and drink beer, cider or cheap wine. We all hated the taste but none of us were prepared to admit it. We'd make up stories about the people who occasionally wandered past us down on the beach, whether they were locals, visitors or dog walkers. All innocent and harmless enough made-up tales but highly amusing to us all at the time.

Most Friday evenings, once we'd finished school when we were younger, and work as we grew older, we'd head to the beach. Marjorie was always dressed impeccably. Hair perfect, lips precisely painted, Trellinick's very own version of Audrey Hepburn

How ironic that the most incredible story was now being played out again from this beach, but this time for real and possibly not that innocent.

It was on this bench with Edwin that I realised that our experimenting with alcohol as youngsters had become a habit which unlike the rest of us, he'd been unable to control. Even after we were married and Sebastian and Chloe were born, he'd sit on this bench after closing time and continue drinking. Eventually he'd wander home, but only once either the screeching of gulls or the chill wind had woken him.

In truth, those nights were the easier ones. The nights where he came straight home from the pub were the ones where his violence was its worst. The children knew from a young age to make themselves scarce. I too would try and limit my interactions with him but if the mood took him, he'd seek one of us out. Thankfully usually me.

I could feel myself growing emotional, so I shuck my head and stood tall against the breeze. I assumed one of Marjorie's Pilates positions and held myself firm. I then did what my therapist suggested I do when he encroached my thoughts when I hadn't invited him to, 'Not now Edwin, you're not stealing another perfect afternoon from me'.

If anyone had been passing by and witnessed my performance, they may have been tempted to phone the men in white jackets, it must have looked and sounded quite unhinged. But I was quite alone but for some distant gulls who busied themselves with matters far more important than a sixty-eight-year-old woman with a long memory.

Stretch complete and mind diverted I wondered how Albert was doing. Sitting in his perfect little home with the glasses perched on his nose wrangling with his favourite daily puzzle. Two men I loved so dearly. One who spread chaos and pain, the other whose job it was to heal it.

I bet Albert worried about us two life-innocent women and the bundle of money which could either make or break us.

I made my way slowly back up the beach. The trees lining the private lane were in full blossom. Pink petals drifting down like confetti, welcoming me home. I slipped through the gate, but before going inside, I stopped at Albert's window.

I knocked gently, not urgent.

"I thought I'd check you hadn't combusted from your own thoughts - or the crossword."

He raised an eyebrow. "Not yet. Bit stuck on seven across but I'll get it."

I allowed myself to walk in and picked up the paper. "'A holiday essential - 5 letters.' Hmm. No idea. Wine is too few letters and condoms is too many. You're on your own chum."

"Hetty, please. I can tell the sorts of holidays you used to enjoy clearly!"

I poured myself a glass of water, gulped it noisily, then rinsed the glass through placing it carefully on the drainer.

"Albert I've just been on the beach, and I was thinking about the money. We've not done anything stupid with it, I said "Not yet. Just so you know. Neither Marjorie nor I have even touched it since the day she found it."

He nodded. "I appreciate that."

We stood quietly in the warmth of his little front room. I looked around, as if the break in silence we were searching for might be hiding in plain sight.

"I've just been to Marjorie's bench," I said. "I'm restless, Albert. It just feels like something's coming."

He smiled. "Well, with you two involved, it usually is."

CHAPTER ELEVEN
Albert

They hadn't done anything yet. I don't know why she made a point of telling me as such, but Hetty had confirmed it. I must remember to tell her, A holiday essential (5 letters) was cream.

The bag still sat beneath Marjorie's bed, untouched. But the idea of it, the presence of it, had already started working its way into the air we breathed.

We were three people holding a match, wondering whether it would burn down a house or light a candle.

Marjorie had gone quiet, which was always telling. She didn't brood aloud. She went inward. And Hetty, she was more vocal than ever, which meant she was trying not to feel something.

We'd agreed to wait seven days. It had only been five. But the weight of those days was building. They'd held back, yes, but just barely.

I trusted them, of course I did. But I also knew how desperation and regret can reshape a person's sense of right and wrong.

That night, after supper with them both, I made the short journey home slowly through the dark. The cold helped. It cleared my thoughts. Narrowed the noise. It would literally take me a minute from Marjorie's home to mine, but I chose to walk up through the grounds and past the park owners house first. I just appreciated the air.

Once home, I poured myself a glass of brandy and sat down with the notebook I kept but rarely used. Not a journal, I wasn't sentimental enough for that. Just a place to put thoughts that wouldn't stay quiet. Hetty asking me about Kathleen yesterday had rattled me. Not because she'd asked, but because I knew she was right.

I wrote:

"Not every good deed is clean. Not every clean decision is good. The trick is figuring out who you're trying to save, and from what."

I stared at the words for a long time. Then I closed the book.

Kathleen would've scolded me for wallowing. She used to say that sadness was only useful if it led somewhere. But she also used to lie with such gentleness, I almost thanked her for it.

That's the part I still don't understand, how someone can hurt you with love. Not anger. Not cruelty. Just... love, misapplied. She thought she was giving me something I couldn't give myself. A gift. A future.

And in a way, she did.

But some truths, once spoken, stay between you and the silence.

And together, without speaking more, we listened to the quiet.

Not in fear,

but in preparation.

CHAPTER TWELVE
Marjorie

It hadn't just taken up space beneath the bed, it had moved in somewhere inside me too. Made itself at home. I couldn't shake it. Couldn't put it back in the sand where I'd found it.

It was here now.

And so was everything it had stirred up.

I told Hetty I couldn't stop thinking about William.

She didn't flinch. She never did, not when it mattered.

"You always do, Marjorie. I do understand, honey," she said gently.

"I know. But this is different. It's louder this time."

Hetty nodded. "The bag's made everything louder. I said this to Albert yesterday. I think we're out of our depth with it all. We came to Beachcombers for sanctuary and peace. Then, like a bolt out of the blue, a small fortune lands on your beach. It's no surprise it's upset you, Marjorie. It really isn't."

I didn't speak. Just stared into my tea until the steam blurred my eyes, or maybe it was tears.

"But why am I relating it to William, Hetty? Yes, I do always think of him. Christ, there isn't a day goes by where I don't think of him. But this is different. I keep replaying it all. Telling my excuse of a mother I was pregnant. Do you remember that day, Hetty?"

"Like I could ever forget, Marj."

"I lie in bed and replay it, over and over in my mind. The kitchen. The stone floor. The way she looked at me like

I was something she was ashamed of."

Hetty reached across the table and squeezed my hand.

"We were all eighteen, Hetty. What the hell did any of us know about life? Why didn't she just say we'd sort it out? That a new life in the house would be a blessing after Dad's death. Why did she have to react the way she did?"

"What was she doing before you told her?"

"She was ironing in the kitchen. I told her straight - we'd practised it a dozen times at your house, if you remember."

"I'm pregnant."

She didn't stop what she was doing. Just pressed the iron into my father's shirt like it was a punishment. A shirt she knew there was sadly no prospect of him ever wearing again.

Silence.

Then she rounded on me:

"You stupid, stupid girl. You and this Michael - children, nothing more than stupid children messing in an adult world. Now this. Don't even dare to describe this as love, Marjorie. Call it what it is. A mess."

I blinked. "Mum…."

"Your father's barely cold in the ground. People are being kind to you and me. Rallying around us at this difficult time and this is how you repay them? How you repay me? You wanted attention and now look."

"It's not like that."

"You think this is love? You think this is what your father would've wanted?" She spat the words. Turned the iron off with a flick that nearly toppled it.

"I didn't do this for attention."

She approached me then, uncomfortably close. Threatening.

"You have no morals. No shame. A child out of wedlock, what kind of life do you think you're giving it? You'll ruin your future, and you'll drag our family name down with you. If you think for one second you'll be playing happy families in this house, well, you've another thing coming. What a stupid, stupid mistake, Marjorie."

The blood pounded in my ears. My throat burned.

"My baby is not a mistake," I said, through tears I couldn't stop. "He was made from love. He is love."

Silence.

Her jaw set like stone.

"Stop. You know nothing about love. Selfishness, yes. But love? I will take care of this mess like I have every mess we've been in," she said coldly. "Discreetly."

I don't remember what I said after that.

Maybe nothing.

Maybe everything I could never take back.

But I remember walking out.

I remember the wind, how it stole my breath.

I remember you answering the door in your slippers and letting me in without asking a single question.

You were the only one I ever told.

The only one who held my shaking hands as the rest of my life rearranged itself.

But Hetty. I'm done with crying. I can't listen to Violets vile rant in my head anymore. I'm just done with it.

Hetty passed me a tissue without a word, taking one for herself at the same time.

She didn't need words.

We'd lived this together.

Hetty stayed with me until I'd gathered myself. She knew the right things to say, and the right time to say them. It had been a dance we'd mastered our whole lives. She'd sink and I would be there to help her swim again. She always did the same for me.

That night, I sat on the edge of my bed and pulled the bag out.

Not to count the money.

Not to dream of the wealth I could now claim I had.

I just wanted to feel it.

To feel its weight against my knees.

To prove to myself one more time that it was real.

I knew keeping the money was not right.

But I'd spent my entire life doing "right," and where had that got me?

No, this time, I was going to do what was right for me.

Hopefully, what was right for the three of us.

I had a plan for it.

I just hoped the others were having the same ideas.

CHAPTER THIRTEEN
Hetty

We were into day six.

Six days since she found the bag. Since we sat in her living room like a pair of shell-shocked children, staring at a fortune we didn't ask for and didn't know what to do with.

Albert had said to wait. One week. Let it breathe. Let it settle. He really was the calm to the storm we both seemed trapped in. We had hoped that knowing what lay under Marjorie's bed would bring clarity, a decision we could all live with.

But nothing had settled, least of all our nerves. We were still on high alert. Every car pulling into the park, every call from an unknown number, every visitor crossing the grounds felt like a potential claimer of the money.

For the first few days, Albert and I had accompanied Marjorie to the beach in the morning. I knew she hated it, but we felt better at her side, just in case.

By day four, she drew the line. Said she was going it alone. She hadn't appreciated my rape alarm, my morning energy, or my tea (rude). Had she known about the kitchen knife in my rucksack, I doubt she would have appreciated that either. Not that I'd have used it, but the threat might have bought us time.

The rhythm of our lives had shifted, all within a week. I was looking forward to the day when Marjorie's bed went back to being a place of sanctuary, not a hiding place for questionable cash.

The bag was still under there, wrapped in towels like a sick dog no one knew how to help. I hadn't asked if she'd opened it again. I didn't need to. She had the look of someone keeping secrets from herself.

I made us toast. She didn't want it, but with me stood over her, she ate it.

She sat, hands curled around her teacup like it might anchor her to something real.

I watched her and thought, not for the first time, how lucky we were to have each other. No one alive knew me better than Marjorie, and I could say the same about her. Our lives were stitched together.

The money had unsettled her because for entire life has she represented all that is good. If we were still school children, I guess she'd be the 'goody two shoes' in the class. We're not school children and she still is 'Little Miss Perfect Pants.'

Marjorie Hepburn doesn't do this sort of thing. Her life now revolves around teaching Albert and I how to bake, grow herbs, tidy borders and shop kindly; supporting local business' and not harming the environment. Not clandestine activities of a possibly criminal nature.

That's the problem for her. The easiest thing would be to march into Trellinick Police Station and hand it over. She'd be doing herself a favour, and giving the two officers who man the place, the most interesting day of their careers.

But, and it's a big but, this money also represents an opportunity. One she's never had.

She hasn't said it, but I knew.

You don't have a friend for over sixty years and not know how their mind works.

Yesterday, when she retold the night she told Violet she was pregnant, I heard something new in her voice. Something resolute, even with the tears.

I've thought of that night too. Two best friends, curled into each other. One broken by cruelty, the other by helplessness.

It wasn't just hard on Marjorie. Michael remained oblivious of this unfolding story, and I thought that was terribly unfair. He'd left Trellinick before she realised she was pregnant. I begged her to tell him. His mother was still in the village. She could get a message to him. He deserved to know.

But Marjorie, ever selfless, wouldn't do it. Said she wouldn't bring that heartache to his door. He had made it clear his future lay elsewhere. That he no longer belonged to her, or to Trellinick.

He had loved her. That was certain. But Exeter beckoned, and his life moved on.

That night, we fell asleep like spoons. My hands in hers. Hers resting on the swell of her belly.

It's one of two nights I'll never forget.

The other is harder to speak about.

The night I found out what Edwin had done.

I was in the hallway at St Michael's, still wearing the coat I'd rushed out in. The nurse was kind, too kind. That tilted-head voice they use when the truth is coming. She guided me into a side room and closed the door quietly. The clean, antiseptic smell didn't match what I feared I was about to hear.

"He's stable," she said. "But... I'm so sorry, Hetty, there's something else. There was another car. A fatality. The police will need to speak to you. Will you take a seat?"

Fatality.

Such a clean word for such a ruin.

He had been drinking again. But this time, he hadn't just screamed, or swung, or passed out on the doorstep. This time, he had taken a car that wasn't his and killed a man who was simply in the wrong place.

I didn't cry. I nodded, sat in the plastic chair, and realised I'd never be able to explain to my children how the man they loved had shattered someone else's family. I was there, but not. Staring at the flicker of light on the officer's radio. A vacant version of myself answered their questions.

When they'd finished, the nurse, her uniform starched, immaculate, offered to take me to Edwin. I refused. It wasn't just that I didn't want to see him. I couldn't trust what I might do if I did.

Later, as I left the hospital, it hit me. The hurt, the shame, the weight of a life so full of promise, lying in a bed guilty of taking another life.

I sobbed uncontrollably as I reached the doors. I steadied myself against the wall. Strangers looked on as the breezed past me laden with flowers and treats for their loved ones.

My legs wouldn't move.

Then arms wrapped around me. Familiar. Warm.

Marjorie.

My harbour.

"Come on, sweetie. Let's get you home. You don't have to talk, that can wait."

To this day, I don't know how she knew where I was. Maybe one of the children. I never asked, and they've never said.

In the car, we didn't speak. I leaned my head against the window and silently wept. For the sadness. For the chaos. For the loneliness.

He died a few days later. Just like that.

People said I was free. I knew in time I would recognise that too. The fantasy I'd had about him disappearing forever was now a reality. I didn't feel the relief I'd aways believed I would.

Grief doesn't follow logic. Sometimes it clings to who someone could have been. Sometimes it waits, quiet and coiled, until a smaller grief lets it rise again.

I didn't tell Marjorie everything. Not the worst parts. But she knew the shape of it. She'd seen the bruises. Seen the way I flinched when the phone rang late.

We've carried each other, in our own ways.

But now, as I sat in her living room, I saw her holding something back. I saw it. The tiniest glint of something in the girl I once wrapped in blankets.

Now sitting over a fortune.

Under her bed.

Had she made a plan for it?

CHAPTER FOURTEEN
Albert

The bag hadn't been mentioned, but it hovered.

I could feel it in the pauses.

In the way Hetty lit a second candle at supper, like distraction might soften the edges.

In the way Marjorie kept apologising for absolutely everything, when there was absolutely nothing to apologise for.

We'd agreed to wait seven days.

The morning would bring the seventh.

No one said it aloud.

I left that evening, as did Marjorie, several glasses deep.

It was as if by eating and drinking too much, we'd managed to avoid the elephant in the room. Or the bag under the bed.

Supper was good. Roast chicken. Hetty swore it wasn't shop-bought (it was), but I wasn't really hungry.

Back at home, I poured a whisky and sat in the chair by the window.

The one I never quite call Kathleen's, but still feel bad sitting in.

She never actually lived here.

But I still catch myself expecting her to walk through the door, laughing too loudly, dropping her scarf, kicking off her shoes like she always did.

Kathleen had a presence.

People said she moved like a dancer. Not the slow, floaty

kind - but the fierce, high-kicking kind you see in Riverdance. She had that kind of poise. Back straight. Hands expressive. Hair a little wild. Eyes that could flick from mischief to fire in a blink.

She was the most alive person I'd ever met.

Her childhood was storybook chaos, Galway hills, too many cousins, fires that never went out.

There was a drink for every occasion in that house: whiskey for nerves, sherry for comfort, Guinness for strength.

And always music. Someone humming, someone banging out reels on a tinny piano or fiddle. Dancing badly in the hallway.

She once told me her father proposed to her mother halfway through a céilí and forgot to stop dancing.

I believe it.

My upbringing was quieter. Straighter.

My father worked in finance. My mother ironed pillowcases and corrected grammar at the table.

We loved each other, but it was a love you could miss if you weren't paying attention.

It was a traditional English version of love – stiff, focused and not overly demonstrative. As opposed to the Irish version of love, which was warm, exaggerated and constant.

Kathleen herself was a hurricane in high heels. Perhaps the perfect metaphor of her upbringing.

She made people laugh. Made rooms feel warmer.

She had friends everywhere, at work, on trains, in post office queues. Strangers told her their life stories in cafés. She had that face. That openness.

She was, irritatingly, brilliant at everything.

By thirty, she was a respected solicitor with a laugh that echoed through three rooms.

And she loved me.

I never quite understood why, but she did.

We had our little circle back then.

Dinners. Weekends away. Birthdays with too much

wine and music in kitchens.

Most of all, there were the McBride's.

Harvey and Morag.

They lived two doors down from us in Abbotsworth, just outside Bath.

Morag was Scottish, sharp and wry, always in oversized jumpers. Kathleen adored her. They were thick as thieves. Long walks. Endless mugs of tea.

Harvey and I got on too, though I never quite matched his boisterousness.

He hugged too hard. Always brought two bottles of wine. Loud, kind, open-hearted.

We were both doctors, I was a GP, he a consultant cardiologist, but his loudness filled rooms in ways I never could.

It wasn't unkind. It just wasn't me.

His brother Charlie was the same.

Only Charlie had the added advantage of being handsome and single.

Sometimes I think those were the best years.

Before things shifted.

Before the night in a hospital when silence arrived like a scalpel.

We don't talk about that now.

Kathleen and I still speak, now and then.

But I feel sure she senses what I feel. Our conversations are stiff, polite, impersonal.

I sipped my whisky and thought of my two friends.

Of the way grief takes shape in different people.

Marjorie wears hers like a soft coat.

Hetty stitches jokes over the holes.

I keep mine folded away in a drawer, mostly.

The money hadn't changed them yet.

But it would. I had to hope that change was for the better. That something good would come of it. Why shouldn't it. We were all dabbling in the 'the dark arts' keeping the money, but sometimes in life, an opportunity presents itself and you just have to run with it.

I did what I always do when things feel unsteady.
I made a list:
Day seven
No decision made
Bag still hidden
Marjorie thinner in spirit
Hetty covering too much with too little
I am sure my plan matches Hetty's
I closed the notebook.
Sat in the dark a little longer.
I wished, just once, that Kathleen would walk through the door, scarf in hand, fire in her eyes, and tell me what the hell we were supposed to do now.

CHAPTER FIFTEEN
Marjorie

D-Day.

Day seven.

I woke before the alarm, which is saying something, as last night's "little supper and drink" at Hetty's ended up being a lot later, and a lot boozier, than planned. My chest felt tight, not with fear, but with certainty. The kind that doesn't wait for permission.

I stuck to my usual routine, knowing full well that Hetty wouldn't be stirring early, not after the amount of wine she'd put away. I now feared hearing Ed Sheeran songs, having endured far too many "Hetty renditions" the night before, thanks to Albert's new Spotify app.

My mobile phone is ancient. I've no idea if it can even use apps, but if it can, I'm getting Albert's Emily to put Spotify on it. What a joy, open access to any music I fancy.

I made tea, toasted my teacakes, packed them into my bag, and got myself ready for the morning walk to my bench. As I pottered about, gathering keys, scarf, coat, I kept glancing at the bag under the bed, as if it might vanish before I had the chance to do something right with it.

Later.

We'd decide later.

The wind was bracing, but calmer than the mornings that had greeted me all week. A sign, I hoped, of calmer days ahead for me too.

I gazed across the empty beach. Reassuringly empty. The grasses on the dunes still frantically folded and tangled into one another as I placed my cushion down and turned on the radio. The steam from my tea veered sharply right with the breeze, so I drank it quickly. Lukewarm tea would've felt like a defeat.

This had been our beach. The dunes, our playground. First as innocent children, and later, to my great cost, something far less innocent.

It pains me to call it that, a cost, but that's what it became. Something I paid for, quietly, for decades.

How strange that our lives unfolded without the other knowing. Mine, haunted by a decision made without my consent. His, untouched by it, the cruellest irony of all.

Michael paid a price too. He was robbed of the chance to know what we had created. Robbed of the choice to be part of it. Worst of all, he never even knew what had been taken from him.

I caught the tears forming, the lump rising in my throat, before they turned into something more painful. I wiped my face, stood, let the wind tussle my hair, and took a long sip of tea.

I reminded myself I had my health, my home, my wonderful friends. I just wished I could be free, finally free of this invisible pain that still lingered.

I sat again and thought back to Hetty's antics the night before. Replaying her irreverent behaviour after a few glasses of wine was always a good antidote to my emotional grey clouds.

She battles her own storm.

She always has.

Hetty is a master at hiding pain, and at coming to the aid of others. But I know it's there. Always.

She worries about me more than she'll admit. Months after Edwin died, we were sat together in a tea shop overlooking the harbour in Padstow. She reached for my hand. She said that while she grieved the man she'd married, and the life she'd lost, she grieved for me differently.

"Because your story has no ending." she said. "That's the cruelty of it. I know where Edwin is. He's gone, and he can't come back. But you... you don't know where William is. Or if he even thinks of you."

That's Hetty.

Wild. Unfiltered. Erratic. Endlessly selfless.

I knew what she'd endured. The sleepless nights spent comforting her children after Edwin's drunken rages. The bruises. The broken furniture. The stolen cash.

I never pried, but I saw more than she realised. I gave her space and dignity when she needed it. And when she let me in, I was there for her.

She was embarrassed, not of Edwin exactly, but of the way he'd made her shrink. It was drunk Edwin who had brought shame on her beautiful little family. Hetty saw the looks from neighbours and so-called friends at the school gates. She heard the gossip.

She knew I didn't judge her. And still, she tried to protect me from the worst of it.

But I knew.

Everyone knew.

I gathered my flask, radio, and cushion, and made my way home.

It was nine thirty.

Almost time for the meeting. Not quite the war office, but it felt close.

The decision wasn't final yet, but I had my thoughts. And I hoped my partners in crime were on the same page.

By ten o'clock, Hetty and Albert were in my lounge. No ceremony, just three friends and a shared secret. Sitting on sofas. Trying to be calm. Each of us waiting for the other to begin.

"Right then," Hetty said, kicking off her slippers.

"Let's find your boy."

CHAPTER SIXTEEN
Hetty

It was happening.

Day Seven. Decision day. The day we either returned the money to the dunes, handed it over to the police, or did what we all secretly really wanted, keep it.

We were in Marjorie's living room. Her place always made big decisions feel more formal, probably because her cushions were aligned and her teapot matched the cups. Albert sat in the armchair like it was a board meeting and he was clearly Chair. Marjorie was perched on the edge of the sofa, wringing her hands.

I had brought my ridiculous squeaky pen and a pad I had labelled Operation Tiffany.

I broke the silence.

"Right then. Let's find your boy."

"Albert and I have chatted. We thought we should employ a private detective to find William, put that money to good use. We had researched one in London who specialised in this very scenario."

Marjorie looked up.

"We're keeping it. A private detective? This is all so very cloak and dagger. I'm so relieved. I was thinking the very same. I didn't know how, but I hoped we could use the money to find William. I wonder if this was fate. I found the money, but we all had the same plan for it. I'm just so nervous. What if it comes back to bite us."

There was a pause.

Albert leaned forward, voice low and kind.

"It's alright to be nervous, Marjorie. You wouldn't be you if you weren't. I'm sure we've all done a lot of thinking this week. Like Hetty just said, maybe it's time to stop thinking, or overthinking, and start doing."

She let out a breath that sounded more like a sigh of surrender.

"I just keep thinking," she said, "what if someone comes? What if we're doing something awful?"

"We're not," I said firmly. "No one's missing this money. No one's asked. No police, no posters, no scandal in the local paper. It's been a week. It's yours now. No offence, Marj, but that bench of yours is hardly a tourist hot spot. I'm convinced it was left there for you. God only knows why, but it was."

I felt myself on a roll then.

"Look at it another way. Say that money was part of some sort of a crime. I don't know, a drugs deal, or a payment for a hitman - unlikely but stay with me here. You, or if it makes you feel better, we, are taking the proceeds of crime and converting them into the proceeds of good. You are a modern-day version of Robin Hood and we're your Merry Men!"

Albert nodded slowly, I think in agreement. "Interesting take on matters as always Hetty, but I see your point."

"Whatever the reason it ended up by your bench, I believe it was meant for you. And even if I didn't, I've seen what it's stirred in you. You're changing, Marjorie. There's a spark in you and I love it.

Your mother, or should I say Violet, for reasons I will never understand, made a decision that shaped your entire life. Here you are, with your two best friends. Friends who love you, who want the best for you. Let's start the reshape, Marjorie. Who knows where this search will take you. For once in your life, Marjorie May Hepburn, dip your toe in, old girl. Do something for you."

She looked at Albert. Then at me.

"Thank you, Albert. Hets. I know you're both right... but I still feel a bit panicky."

"Perfectly normal," he said. "But don't let it stop you."

"You've earned this," I added. "And what's more, you're not doing anything selfish with it. We're finding your son."

She blinked, visibly holding back tears.

"Oh, and another thing," I added with a grin, "we're going to London. Breakfast at Tiffany's," I said, half laughing, half terrified, looking at the shock on Marjorie's face.

"Harrods, darling. Audrey would approve. You in your pearls, me in my gloves, looking fabulous. I've seen it in your magazine, the Breakfast at Tiffany's experience at Harrods. That's a little bit of us, don't you think?"

Albert was grinning and winked at Marjorie.

"I expect a postcard. And maybe a scone?"

Marjorie relaxed a little then. She hugged us both.

"I can't believe we've decided. I'm so relieved. I've been so worried you wouldn't think I should keep it."

"I'm still scared," she added quietly.

"That's alright," Albert said gently. "But you're not alone."

That's when we heard tyres on gravel.

Marjorie stiffened. Albert glanced up from his tea. I instinctively reached for the nearest heavy object, which happened to be my notebook. Useless, but symbolic.

The three of us were at the window like meerkats. A car none of us recognised, driven by a man in a suit and sunglasses on an overcast day, with a young woman in business attire riding passenger.

A car door slammed. Footsteps. Crunching. Slow. Deliberate.

We watched them from behind Marjorie's heavy curtains. They were purposefully walking straight for her front door.

Knock.

Three raps. Polite, but official.

"Oh God," Marjorie breathed.

"Stay calm," Albert murmured, voice steady. "The money hasn't been touched. If it's the police, we simply hand it over. You've been unwell and hadn't managed to hand it over yet."

Marjorie stood, every inch of her vibrating, and pulled the door open just a crack.

The man stood on the step, mid-fifties, lean, dressed in a navy mac that looked like it had seen both rain and surveillance. Sunglasses removed. He carried a clipboard and had a lanyard tucked awkwardly into his jacket.

"Mrs Hepburn?" he asked smiling too broadly. "Apologies for the intrusion. I'm Councillor Brearley from the local authority, this is Clara, my assistant. We're gathering views on the A38 bypass proposal. Just wondering if you might have five minutes?"

Marjorie didn't answer for a moment. Her mouth opened, then closed again. Her hand stayed on the edge of the door like it was the only thing holding her up.

"Now's... not a good time," she managed. "I've got some neighbours here and we're chatting about plans to go to London. Not for anything in particular. Just a little trip away. A treat, you might say. Just me and Hetty, Albert isn't coming. Harrods, possibly a gallery or two, Buckingham Palace... that kind of thing."

"Of course. How exciting. London is a wonderful city, a far cry from sleepy Cornwall. I'll leave a leaflet," he said quickly, already reaching for it. "We're just engaging with the community. I'll leave a couple for your neighbours too. Any questions, just give us a call or drop me an email."

Marjorie nodded once. "Right. Thank you."

She took the leaflets, closed the door gently. Not slammed, not rude. Just firm.

The silence in the room was thunderous.

I let out the breath I'd been holding.

Then I whispered, "Holy shit. I thought that was CID. Christ, Marjorie, you virtually told him the whole itinerary. I was waiting for, oh yes, councillor, I found a mysterious bag of money on the beach and now I'm blowing it on a trip to Harrods. Fancy joining us?"

Marjorie laughed, "He looked like a bloody detective. I

just panicked."

"He had clipboard energy," I said. "Like someone trained in passive-aggressive arrest strategy."

Albert sipped his tea. "Possibly the least threatening man I've ever seen. But yes, unfortunate timing."

"Unfortunate?" I hissed. "He nearly sent me into cardiac arrest with his bloody infrastructure reforms. I was on the brink of asking for a spare pair of pyjama bottoms Marjorie!"

Marjorie managed another watery laugh. "I don't even know what the A38 is."

"Doesn't matter," I said, waving the leaflets. "We are clearly on some cosmic watchlist. And now your opinion on roadworks is public record."

Albert leaned back in his chair. "Well. If we weren't sure before, I think we are now."

Marjorie frowned. "Sure, of what?"

"That we're doing the right thing," he said gently. "And that maybe it's time to stop flinching at shadows."

Marjorie looked at both of us. Then down at the leaflets. "So, we go to London to meet a private detective, have lunch at Harrods dressed like Audrey Hepburn, all on money that could have been used in a crime.?"

"Yes. That's about the sum of it."

She looked to us both. Then, finally, she laughed uncontrollably. In fact, we all did. Rather embarrassingly, I laughed so uncontrollably I ended up needing those spare pyjama bottoms. I really must get my pelvic floor sorted out.

CHAPTER SEVENTEEN
Marjorie

I didn't sleep much that night. The kind of sleep where you hover just beneath the surface, never really falling, never really rising.

The leaflet from the councillor was still on the kitchen counter, folded twice with precision, as if tidiness might undo the panic it had caused.

It hadn't.

By morning, the world had righted itself. Sort of. The sun came up over Trellinick Bay. The gulls screeched as they always did. The waves pulsed in and out as if breathing - a gentle consistency I needed. I didn't stay long. I sipped my tea and nibbled at my teacake but didn't linger. The shipping forecast could wait. I packed my bag up, checked the beach was once again devoid of a person or persons looking for a lost bag and content the coast was clear, walked home.

As I walked through the gate, Hetty waved a fresh loaf at me from across the way. Albert brought milk.

We didn't talk about the councillor at the door, or the fear that had closed around my throat like a net. We just had tea and toast and chatted about the impending trip.

But something had shifted. Not in the world, in me.

I'd said yes.

Not out loud. Not on a form. But to something bigger. I'd said yes to the possibility that I could still act, still matter, still find him.

William.

Even thinking his name felt different now. Less like an

open wound, more like the memory of one. The scar still itched. But it no longer bled.

I busied myself with practical things. Washed the sheets. Took inventory of the fridge. Tried on three different scarves for a trip I still hadn't even packed for.

London? A private detective? What on earth was happening to me, to my simple little life?

I hadn't been to London in years. Maybe decades. Not since Hetty's children were young and we took them to see Big Ben. I imagined us, Hetty and me, standing outside Harrods, pretending to be Audrey and Grace Kelly, dragging Albert's ghost with us via postcard.

I didn't let myself think too hard about what would happen if our detective found him. What I would say. What he would think. That way led to paralysis. I locked away in a secret room in my brain the possibility that there was no William - that the very worst had happened. Or that there was still a William, but he had no interest in meeting me.

Instead, I held on to something else, the knowledge that, this time, I wasn't letting silence win.

I stood at the back window and looked out at the sea, the low dunes, the pale green of spring trying to break through.

This was the beach of Michael and me. The place where innocence had been made and lost. The place where something had begun, even if it had taken a lifetime to understand what.

The bag still sat under my bed. I hadn't moved it since Day One.

And now, I didn't need to.

Because what had once felt like a burden now felt like permission.

We were going to London.

We were going to find William.

And I was finally ready to be found, too.

Later that afternoon, I walked down to the bench.

My bench.

The breeze had picked up, and the tide was folding in,

slow and persistent. I sat with my coat wrapped tightly around me, the bag left behind in the house. I didn't need it here.

This was the place I came when I couldn't carry the pain of losing him anymore. When memory pressed too close to the surface.

And today, I let it rise.

I remembered that morning.

The morning my mother took him from me.

William was just days old. Still soft and blinking, uncertain of the world. I remember the weight of him in my arms, how he fit perfectly into the curve of my chest. His smell, milk and warmth and something inexplicably pure. His fingers curled tightly at first, then unfurled as he slept, one tiny hand slipping free of the blanket as she reached for him.

She didn't speak. Just nodded to the vicar beside her. He stood there like some holy escort, pretending this was mercy. But there was no grace in that moment. Only removal. And I hated them both for it.

I must have begged her not to do it. But the words have blurred with time.

What I remember most is the sound of him, that small, helpless cry as he left the room. Not distressed. Just surprised. Like the world had shifted before he understood how.

Hetty saw them. She was walking by the church. She saw my mother carrying the bundle that was my son, clutched in her arms like laundry.

Hetty didn't know what to do. None of us did. She was just there, like she always was when I needed her, a heart beating in a room where mine had been broken.

She found me, slumped in the corner of my bedroom, holding the teddy bear she'd bought him. The soft blue one. The first gift. The last gift. The scent of him, my only comfort.

I don't remember much after that. Just the silence. The unbearable silence of a baby no longer there.

All I was told was that he was going to a couple in Norfolk. That they were good people. That he would have a better life.

Better than me, apparently.

I never knew their names. Never saw papers. Never had a number to call. Just an empty cot, a bedroom that smelled of talc and grief, and a silence that lasted decades.

I could still scream against the injustice of it all. The cold, cruelty of it. How many tears had I shed for my boy?

I sat motionless as my thoughts were lost to him.

The waves rolled in.

I stayed until dusk.

Because remembering him fully, his weight, his sound, his leaving, felt like part of finding him again.

And I would find him.

I had no idea what I'd say.

But I'd know him.

I'd know.

CHAPTER EIGHTEEN
Albert

Kathleen used to say I was too fond of silence. That I hoarded it, like other men hoarded tools or golf clubs. I think she meant it affectionately. Though sometimes, I wasn't sure.

We hadn't actually spoken in months. That was our rhythm now, absence softened by the occasional WhatsApp, an obligatory text about Emily. But even distance doesn't erase history.

It was always the betrayal that caught people by surprise. That our marriage ended not in shouting, not in another woman, but in something quieter. A secret she thought was kindness. A lie that began in love.

I still loved her.

That was the hardest part.

I had wanted to give her everything, just not like that.

I looked at the photograph still framed on my shelf. The three of us at Polzeath beach. Emily's curls stuck to her cheeks. Kathleen caught mid-laugh. I used to think the photo was tainted. Now, I'm not so sure. There was love in it, even if some of it had been built on broken ground.

And love counts.

Even if it doesn't last the way we imagined.

Kathleen was always in motion. Her work as a solicitor spilled into everything; long hours, late meetings, endless people who needed her. And she liked it that way. She once told me stillness made her nervous.

"Still things get dusty," she said, laughing.

Kathleen and Morag were like sisters. They hit it off instantly. There was no professional overlap, Morag was an interior designer, but their friendship was fast, deep, and full of shared weekends, theatre trips, shopping sprees. A closeness that, once formed, became immovable.

Charlie McBride often joined us, Harvey's younger brother. Charlie was everyone's favourite. Too handsome for his own good. Too clever to be ignored. And always a little too interested in other men's wives.

He flirted with Kathleen in that effortless, supposedly harmless way that certain men never outgrow. Late-night debates about politics or philosophy that always seemed to end in shared laughter and another glass of something expensive.

I never worried. I never thought I needed to.

Kathleen would brush it off with a smile.

"He's all theatre," she'd say. "You're the one I come home with, wake up next to, and share morning coffee with. Do you think I haven't met a thousand Charlie McBride's in my time Albert? I've got his card marked. Please don't ever worry on that score. I'm as big a flirt as he is."

And I believed her.

I had no reason not to.

We were solid, I thought. Built on honesty, loyalty, and hard-won affection.

But in hindsight, there were glances I should have noticed. Silences I explained away. A weight to their laughter that, once remembered, no longer sits quite right.

We saw much less of Charlie once Kathleen became pregnant with Emily, and Morag with Oliver. I guessed he hadn't found the chatter about impending parenthood as illuminating as the debates he'd so often enjoyed with my wife.

Harvey, Morag, and I would leave them to it, still deep in discussion at the dining table, while we retreated to the lounge to talk about anything but politics or law. Soon enough, Kathleen would wander back through, settle on my lap, and wrap her arms around my shoulders.

I didn't question it.

I Didn't want to.

Sometimes we protect ourselves from the answers we already suspect.

But even the best foundations can have cracks you don't see until it rains.

I glanced out the window.

Marjorie's light was on. She was home safe.

Tomorrow we'd book the train tickets. I wouldn't be going with them - I'd already decided that. London wasn't for me anymore. But I'd be here when they got back. Waiting. Listening. Anchoring.

Because that's what I could offer.

Not answers.

Not money.

Just stillness.

And loyalty.

Sometimes, that's enough.

CHAPTER NINETEEN
Hetty

I didn't sleep.

Not because I was worried about the trip, or the money, or whether we'd find William, though all of that churned in the corners of my brain. No, I didn't sleep because some memories come wrapped in silence, and silence is loudest at night.

Marjorie's light had gone off just after eleven. Alberts even earlier. I sat at my window, tea going cold in my hands (I know, tea, right?), staring out across the quiet lanes of Beachcombers and feeling the old ache rise.

Sometimes I think I've moved on. That I've put Edwin behind me like an old coat, heavy and worn, best left in a dark cupboard. But then, without warning, the memory pushes through.

It wasn't just the night he crashed the car that haunted me most. It was learning who had been in the other car. A man. Thirty-six. Husband. Father of two. Killed instantly.

The hospital had called it a tragedy. The police called it an accident, albeit with charges pending if he pulled through. I called it what it was - a bloody, stupid, selfish waste.

He didn't die that night, Edwin. But something did. Whatever rope had held us together snapped for good. And I didn't mourn him, not really. I mourned who I thought he might've been, once. Before the drinking. Before the shouting. Before the bruises we covered with laughter and long sleeves.

He seemed to have no understanding of the pain he

caused us. Not just the physical pain, but the emotional too. The school plays, missed. Parents' evenings, missed. Sebastian's first county cricket match, missed. Chloe chosen to be Rose Queen, missed. And little Connel's first steps, missed.

Why?

Because drink meant more to him than we did. More than anything.

I remember the silence in the house when I got back from the hospital. The children asleep. Not so young anymore, but still innocent. The fridge humming. The smell of bleach still clinging to the kitchen tiles, where I'd scrubbed the night before, like that would fix anything.

I sat on the floor and cried like someone who had finally been given permission.

That was years ago now. But tonight, I felt close to that version of me again. The woman who had wanted something better, but didn't know where to find it, or even what it looked like.

I'm only sixty-eight. Not ready to push the daisies up just yet. I pride myself on my figure, my stylish clothes, and my rustic home-cooked meals (Marjorie would say too rustic). But lately, I'd been feeling... restless.

Marjorie's little windfall had given that restlessness an identity. Had made it three-dimensional, not just a fleeting thought.

This money had rattled something in all of us. Yes, we laughed about it. Plotted with it. But had it awoken more than just the search for William?

My thoughts turned to her.

I pictured her on that beach, carrying grief like glass - polished, but sharp. I thought of the night she told her mother she was pregnant. The storm that followed. The cruelty dressed as righteousness.

I walked into her house the day he was taken. Found her on the floor, cradling the tiny teddy I'd bought for the baby. Her mother had already taken William by then. Just walked out, as if it were her decision to make.

And Marjorie, poor, sweet Marjorie, had sat there

hollowed out. Too quiet even to cry.

She looked broken.

But not anymore.

Next week, we'd board a train to London. We'd sit in a café in Harrods. Play Audrey and Grace Kelly. Pretend we belonged among all that velvet and sparkle.

And then we'd find a man who once had a tiny hand that slipped out from a blanket on a winter morning, and a cry that sounded like hope.

Because Marjorie deserved that.

And, just maybe, I deserved it too.

CHAPTER TWENTY
Marjorie

We gathered at Hetty's home just after ten.

I brought pastries.

Albert brought his laptop.

Hetty brought enthusiasm, a notepad full of dramatic pseudonyms in case we needed one, and a pot of coffee strong enough to resuscitate the dead. Naturally I declined the coffee and made myself a nice pot of English breakfast tea.

Her place was always slightly chaotic. A cushion on every surface. Books stacked like barricades. An array of toys, paint, and white wine. But it had heart. It always had heart. That was what I loved about it. I obviously couldn't live with the chaos and clutter, but it perfectly suited her and that was good enough for me.

I noticed her Norah Jones album was out, which probably meant she'd had a tricky night. I didn't ask, but as she passed with mugs, and a cup and saucer for me, I gave her arm a little squeeze. The faint smile she gave me told me I was right.

"Right," she said, clapping her hands like we were launching a rocket. "To business."

We sat around the kitchen table, me, Hetty, Albert.

Joint conspirators.

We looked at the blank email draft glowing on Albert's screen:

To: Harry.Stavely@PI.co.uk

"I don't have much," I said, already feeling the guilt rise.

"That's alright," Albert replied, fingers poised over the keys.

"All I really know is his name, William Anchorage, and his date of birth. I felt it was right for him to have his father's name. That way, Michael would be part of his son's life, even if he knew nothing of it."

I paused. "Violet was furious when she saw what I had done. But that was one piece of her vile puzzle she couldn't change, his birth certificate. I don't even know if he kept his name. I suspect his surname, at least, may have changed. She told me he was being taken to a couple in Norfolk. That's all I was ever told."

Hetty reached for my hand and gave it a squeeze. "It's more than nothing. It's a start."

Albert nodded. "We'll write what we have. The investigator will ask questions. That's what he's for."

So, we wrote it.

Dear Mr Stavely,

My name is Marjorie May Hepburn. I'm trying to find someone I lost many years ago, well, not lost… had stolen many years ago.

I watched the words appear on the screen. Neat. Plain. Terrifying.

Once it was done, Albert read it aloud one last time. Then, with a glance at me for permission, he hit send.

I felt it like a jolt.

Not the email.

The act of letting the past move forward.

We sat in silence for a moment; the kind only old friends can share without needing to fill.

"One week," Hetty said finally, standing to refill our drinks. "That's what he said. He'd need a few days to get started."

"A week," I repeated. "What is it with seven days and us at the moment?"

It felt impossibly close, and impossibly far, all at once.

Hetty leaned against the counter and took a bite of her almond croissant like it owed her money.

"So, in the meantime. We shop. We pack. We emotionally prepare."

"We haven't booked accommodation yet," I said cautiously. "And we need to talk about how much we spend. How much of this cash do we take with us?"

Albert reached into his inside jacket pocket and handed me a small envelope. My name was written on it in his careful, slanted script.

"What's this?"

"Just read it."

I opened it.

Inside was a printout. A hotel confirmation. Three nights. The Savoy. Two adjoining rooms.

I stared at it. "Albert…"

"It's already done," he said gently. "And before you argue, don't. You've both given me more than money ever could. It's a gift. No debate."

"I… I don't know what to say."

Hetty made a dramatic choking sound. "You booked the Savoy? Bloody hell, Albert. I was hoping for a Premier Inn and a cheese toastie."

He smiled. "I thought you might like a little luxury. And Marjorie deserves to feel… special."

I didn't cry. But my throat tightened in that unmistakable way.

Three nights.

Three nights in a hotel I'd only ever seen in films.

To find a boy I'd last held in my arms as a newborn.

I wasn't ready.

But I was willing.

And maybe that was enough.

Albert raised his mug. "To London."

Hetty clinked hers against his. "To breakfast at Tiffany's."

I lifted mine last.

"To William."

CHAPTER TWENTY-ONE
Albert

I looked out the window.

Marjorie's light was on.

She was still awake. Knowing Marjorie she was fretting about the day's events.

Tomorrow, they'd start packing.

I would stay here, with my tea, and my thoughts, and that tightening in my chest that had nothing to do with age, and everything to do with truths still hiding in the dark.

Because the past isn't finished.

Finding the bag had for some reason made us all reflective. It has presented an opportunity for Marjorie to right the most incredibly painful wrong.

Perhaps it was time I did the same. I wasn't getting any younger. Time was marching on.

The money didn't just represent an opportunity; it represented a reset.

I just had to recognise that and if I could, find the courage to act on it.

CHAPTER TWENTY-TWO
Marjorie

I changed the bed linen even though no one was coming.

Dusted the picture frames.

Wiped down the kitchen tiles.

Sprayed everywhere.

I stood in the hallway holding a lemon-scented cloth and realised I had already wiped the light switch twice.

It wasn't nerves, not exactly. Just motion.

Something to do with my hands while my mind spun wider and wider.

The email was sent.

The hotel was booked.

The train times were printed and paperclipped, by Albert, of course.

It was all happening.

But not yet.

We had a week.

And I didn't know what to do with that time.

On Tuesday afternoon, I walked to the bench for the second time that day.

The weather was mild, that strange pause between spring's promise and summer's arrival.

I sat for a long time, just listening to the wind draw lines across the sand.

I thought of Michael.

He left before I even knew I was pregnant.

Only the Lonely

One of those final conversations, the kind where no one really says goodbye, but everything changes anyway.

"I love you," he said. "But this can't be me forever Marjorie."

He gestured toward the future like it was already beyond the horizon.

"My father's set things in motion. I don't have a choice."

He told me to get on with my life.

And then he left for Exeter, to join his father's accountancy firm.

Just like that.

So, I did.

Or tried to.

I told myself it didn't matter, that it had been young love, seaside hearts.

But that was a lie I wore to survive the weeks that followed.

When I missed my period, I thought it was stress.

When I fainted at work and they sent me home, we all assumed I was merely sickening for something.

In a way, I was.

Morning sickness, though I didn't know it yet.

Impending motherhood should be a time of mutual joy. Two people anticipating a baby.

But for me, it came to represent a dark and distressing time.

Any joy I might have felt was torn away.

Not just because of Michael's absence, or his ignorance of it all.

But because of my own mother.

Violet.

Her name feels more accurate than "Mum."

The title never really suited her.

She wore it like a borrowed coat; stiff, unfamiliar, too buttoned-up and undeserving.

Her actions throughout my pregnancy, cold, calculated, haunt me still.

The way she took William from my arms.

The way she handed him over to strangers as if he were nothing more than a parcel to be redirected.

An inconvenience that didn't fit into her life.

To hell with mine.

It was the darkest period of my life.

I never figured out why she was so cruel. Not really.

Maybe I stopped trying.

Maybe I was afraid to find out it wasn't personal, just who she was.

After William was taken, I remained in the house for two more months.

Two long, silent months in a home that no longer felt like mine.

Then Hetty found us a flat.

A little place in Trellinick with yellowing walls and leaky pipes.

Her parents helped us paint and furnish it.

Hetty made it feel light. Happy. Ours.

Violet died eighteen months later.

"Medical complications." No one explained, and I never asked.

I felt numb.

Not relieved.

Not grief-stricken.

Just… blank.

She left no will.

But my father had, and his instructions were clear, the house and all its contents were to be mine.

I was glad to move back in.

Not because of the house itself, but because it felt like a reclaiming.

Hetty had started seeing Edwin by then. Let's just say they were enthusiastic about one another. Loudly. And often.

I very much felt like a third wheel.

Only the Lonely

Hetty really can't do quiet. In anything.

So, I went back.

I should say home, but it didn't feel like home.

Not the warm hug of familiarity a home should represent.

It was the house where everything had happened.

Where everything had been taken from me.

I made it my own, slowly, quietly.

But I never stopped missing my William.

CHAPTER TWENTY-THREE
Marjorie (Violet's Journal)

I sipped tea on my bench on Wednesday morning, listening to the shipping forecast. I don't know why I listen to it. The weather is right in front of me, and I don't understand a word of it anyway. Fastnet. Cromarty. Dogger. Fisher. Nonsense to me, but no doubt vital to a great many others.

Three more days, and Hetty and I would be off on the trip of a lifetime. I hadn't told her yet, but we were travelling to London first class. I had ordered the tickets online with Albert. He's a whizz on his laptop.

He still hadn't heard back from the private investigator, but he was keeping an eye on his email.

I hadn't brought my toasted teacake to the beach. I hadn't felt hungry these last few days. Excitement, no doubt. I certainly didn't feel unwell. Unnerved, yes, but not unwell.

Since my discovery, I'd been more vigilant at the beach. It had been nearly two weeks now, and while I was a little more relaxed, I still looked around more than was customary for me.

The councillor and his leaflet about the A38 had rattled me more than I'd let on to my co-conspirators. I honestly thought they were the police. Well, we all did!

Hetty said she was keeping a journal of our escapades. She might even write a novel about it. I'd insisted she changed all our names and made it clear that the story was fictional. If she hadn't and her author notes were ever lost (this was Hetty we were talking about), that would be game, set and match for the prosecution.

Only the Lonely

The fact she'd used the word journal rather than diary reminded me of the day I found Violet's journal, months after moving back into the house following her death.

I wasn't looking for it. Indeed, I didn't even know it existed. But there it was, in a box of her personal effects.

I flicked through the pages. Recipes. Dates. Schedules. Phone numbers. Addresses. Home budgets and accounts.

Not a diary, clearly.

It was strange, seeing her handwriting again.

I was about to put it back in the box when it slipped from my hands and fell open, the back page exposed.

I picked it up and sat on the bed. A page filled with scribbled insights.

I never wanted to be married.

Not because I regret it. I don't. But saying it, even here, still feels like betrayal.

Henry was kind. Softly spoken. Loyal. A man who saw goodness in people long after they'd stopped showing it. I never loved him. Not the way he deserved. But I married him because I was pregnant, and that's what was done. My mother nodded, the date was moved forward, and a wedding dress was let out rather than taken in.

Marjorie arrived seven months later. A beautiful baby. Healthy. Quiet. Strong.

But I didn't feel what I was supposed to feel.

I cared for her. I did what was expected. But while the village cooed and Henry beamed, I sat up at night and mourned the life I never got to live.

I'd wanted to be a midwife. I'd sent away for the forms. Dreamt of starched white uniforms and steel instruments and babies whose mothers wanted them, prepared for them. Women I could help, not just judge. But that was all gone the moment I realised I was pregnant.

Henry never once made me feel lesser. He adored her. Dotingly so. He'd rock her to sleep, sing to her under his breath. He looked at her the way I'd hoped he might look at me someday.

I think that's where it started, the distance between me and Marjorie.

She had what I never had: unquestioned love. I was useful. She was precious.

I never meant to resent her. But I did.

Not in ways people could see. I brushed her hair. Packed her lunches. Stitched name tags into her school jumpers. But I kept her just far enough away that she couldn't bruise the parts of me still aching.

She reminded me of youth. Of risk. Of how a single choice could erase the whole map of a woman's life.

When she started seeing that Anchorage boy, I saw history lining itself up again. The glances. The secrets. The foolish belief that love could rewrite consequences.

I watched her fall. And I felt that same old dread press in around my ribs.

I wanted to save her. Truly. But part of me also wanted her to understand. To know what it meant to lose everything before you even knew what you had.

That's the truth I've never said aloud.

She wasn't a mistake.

But she was a cost.

I was stunned. How dare she.

How could she put into writing something she could never bring herself to tell me? How dare she leave it somewhere knowing I would find it someday?

What a thoughtless, cowardly thing to do.

How close to her passing did she write all that?

For whose eyes? Mine?

It read less like an explanation and more like a confession.

And if it were a confession, it would take a lot more than three Hail Marys to absolve her of her sins.

I didn't forgive her.

I hated her in life, and I hated her more now in death. William was her grandson. She gave him away to strangers. How could she think that stealing my son would somehow make my life less of a disaster. That it wouldn't be ruined like hers was with an unwanted, unplanned baby.

I have lived my entire adult life with this turmoil. Not because I had a baby, but because I had one and he was taken.

I closed the book and never spoke a word of it to anyone.

It was discarded with the other unwanted belongings of Violet's.

I remember how I felt then.

I didn't want her life story.

Her empty excuses.

I wanted the son she stole from me.

CHAPTER TWENTY-FOUR
Hetty

There's always a point in packing where I lose the will to live.

Usually somewhere between outfit three and shoe pair six, when I realise I've packed nothing suitable and everything too tight. I'm not built for sleek nights away. I'm built for knitwear and indignation.

Still, I was trying.

Two suitcases lay open on the bed, one sensible, one optimistic.

I stared at both like they might start speaking and tell me what to do.

We were really doing this.

London.

The Savoy.

William.

I paused mid-fold and sat down on the edge of the bed, blouse in hand, and just breathed for a second.

Marjorie had been quiet since the journal.

She hadn't said much, just told me, in that voice she uses when she's trying not to unravel. Many years ago, when she'd moved back into her family home, she'd found something of Violet's.

Something that made the past feel worse, and clearer, all at once.

She only told me because I said I was keeping a journal of this whole story. Bad choice of word by me. I wish I'd said keeping notes.

Only the Lonely

I didn't push.

We're past the age of questions.

Sometimes you just make tea and sit in the silence together.

She's brave, Marjorie. Braver than she knows.

Because it's one thing to have a baby taken from you.

It's another to continue to love him, without the prospect or promise of ever holding him again.

I sipped my wine.

Half-past eleven in the morning, but no one was judging. Not in this house.

Edwin used to say I had a high tolerance for chaos.

That's why I stayed with him so long.

He mistook my endurance for acceptance.

I suppose I did too.

That's why I can't let this trip go wrong.

If we get to London and it's a dead end. If Harry has been unable to locate any information. She would be so disappointed.

I don't know what that will do to her.

And I don't know what that will do to me either.

I looked back at the suitcase.

Packed too much.

Forgot the new underwear I'd bought.

Albert had taken delivery of the parcel when it arrived.

I was at the club with Marjorie, losing at bridge.

He popped round with it later that evening, excitedly asking, "What have you been buying?"

I couldn't resist.

I opened the parcel and held up a lace bra, with matching lace knickers.

"Hell's fire, Hetty. It's a bloody good job it's warm, you'll catch your death in them."

"Wait, Albert. Come back. There's more in here!"

Never in the ten years we'd all lived here had Albert left me so fast. "No thank you Hetty, I get the idea."

It made my night.

I chuckled every time I pictured his face.

Classic.

Still, I'd slipped in the silk red scarf.

And the low-cut navy blouse that made my shoulders look vaguely intentional.

I hadn't worn it since last Christmas, but this felt like the time.

Not that I was hoping for anything.

Just... not not hoping.

It's been a long time since someone looked at me like I was anything other than practical.

And maybe I am tired of looking at the two perfect pillows that occupied the right-hand side of my bed.

So yes, I'll dress for dinner at The Savoy.

I'll wear something silly.

Say something outrageous.

And see if anyone remembers that Hetty Harris was once a bloody catch.

London, here we come.

God help it.

Part Two

London

CHAPTER TWENTY-FIVE
Marjorie

I rose at six.

The sun was snaking its way across my bedroom blind.

I got up quickly and pulled on my tracksuit without showering. I'd usually judge Hetty for doing likewise. I would never normally leave the house without a shower, let alone in tracksuit bottoms. But Hetty wouldn't bat an eyelid. An orange eyelid at the moment. She'd put on fake tan rather too liberally and was a glow of orange warmth.

I quietly locked the door and scurried down to my beach.

No tea.

No teacake.

No cushion or radio.

Just me, the waves, and the memories.

I sat and rocked slightly, trying to stop the tears from coming. I was doing it.

I was putting myself first.

I was doing something I'd never thought possible.

There was hope.

Hope that I might find William, or at least, find some trace of him. I wouldn't allow the thought that he may be no longer with us grow in my mind. But the doubt was there, and I had to be prepared for that outcome too.

My stolen boy.

I didn't stay long.

Just long enough to climb up onto my bench and stretch

my arms out into the wind, to let the gusts tangle my hair and challenge my balance.

As if to feel, for just a moment, what freedom might be like.

I shouted William's name into the wind, hoping it would carry it back to me.

That it would carry him back to me.

Never in ten years - no in all my life, had I behaved liked that in public. To stand on my bench and scream like a banshee the name of my only child. It was so liberating.

Exhilarated, I climbed down. Took one last look at the sea. Then walked home.

Hetty and I had counted the money the night before, the first time I'd actually touched it.

We spent over an hour arranging it into neat piles across my living room floor. An unfeasibly expensive carpet emerged, one hundred piles of one thousand pounds, all in twenty-pound notes.

What in the world, of all things holy, had I found?

In the end, we were kneeling on top of it. We caught each other's eyes and burst out laughing. Uncontrollably. Hysterically. Holding each other, falling across the money like a pair of drunk millionaires.

And then Hetty peed herself.

The sight of her rushing to the bathroom only made me laugh harder, the tangerine dream bolting through my living room, knees bent, arms flailing, clinging to her rapidly departing dignity.

She returned moments later in my clean pyjama bottoms.

"Any chance of a carrier bag, Ronnie Biggs? You won't want my pissy knickers on your floor, will you?"

"Hetty! Honestly! Under the kitchen sink. And wash your hands!"

Crisis resolved, we counted fifteen thousand pounds into a large brown envelope for the private detective. Then set aside another five thousand to take with us. London wasn't cheap.

That left eighty bundles of one thousand pounds.

We decided to hide them in various spots around my house and Hetty's. Albert had a safe, of course, but we didn't want to implicate him any more than we already had.

My Neil Diamond album got two thousand pounds.

So did Abba Arrival and Saturday Night Fever.

My wellington boots became very wealthy.

So did my Bergerac DVDs.

We did the same at Hetty's.

It was my first time exploring her underwear drawer.

Unbelievable!

I had to hope that our memories wouldn't fail us, and we'd be able to locate the money again on our return.

One hundred thousand pounds. On my beach. By my bench. Surely it was a sign.

CHAPTER TWENTY-SIX
Hetty

The morning arrived.

I was both beyond excited and still orange... very orange. As I clambered out of bed, I looked back and noted my crisp white bed sheet also had a tangerine tinge.

I checked one last time that I'd packed my finest clobber. I didn't want Lady Marjorie lecturing me on my attire.

I showered, hoping I would be at least one pantone colour lighter, and dressed to kill in a navy shift dress and pin striped jacket. Make-up perfectly applied and perfume liberally sprayed I felt sure Marjorie would approve. It wasn't every day you got whisked down to London by train to stay at the Savoy.

I looked out the window and saw Albert loading Marjorie's suitcase into the boot of his car. I waved at them, grabbed my own case, jacket and bag, locked the door tightly, and steered my case down the path.

Marjorie had walked back to her house, double-checking that the windows and front door were properly secured. Always the details.

We hugged excitedly and clambered into the back of Albert's car.

"So, ladies," he said, pulling on his seatbelt, "you've got the train tickets, your Savoy confirmation, a fun packed itinerary, Harry's money, your walking shoes, and your broad shoulders?"

We replied check as he worked his way through the list.

A list by the way, that made him sound like a schoolteacher.

"Well, I have exciting news for you both."

I looked at Albert, then grabbed hold of Marjorie's hand.

"I've had a response from Harry. He cut it fine for your trip, but it's something. He has news for you, Marjorie. He wouldn't be more specific, I'm guessing not until he's received payment. It sounds very promising. He'll join you after your breakfast at Tiffany's and tell you everything. Just let him know how that fits into your plans."

Marjorie instinctively put her hand to her mouth and clung to me.

"He has news. Oh, my goodness. I wonder what that means. This is it, Hetty. The whole point of the trip means something now. Harry has news."

We held hands the entire journey to the train station.

Once we'd calmed down a little, Albert kept us entertained with stories about Emily coming to visit him. They were planning to garden, install a small greenhouse to grow herbs, and paint the flaking window frames. He promised to keep a close eye on our homes. He didn't specifically ask where the remaining money was, but we hoped he didn't fancy listening to Majorie's Babara Streisand LP whilst we were gone - the sleeve now contained four thousand pounds.

At the station, we hugged him tightly and promised to keep him updated on our escapades. Then, gathering our cases and bags, we headed off to find our platform. I turned one last time to wave at Albert. His mouthed, "look after her" as he waved to me. I mimed back, "I will, I promise." I turned and picked my way past holiday makers and commuters.

As we stood on the platform, I found myself looking at Marjorie and smiling. For at least the tenth time, she was checking her bag for everything on Alberts list. She was also checking out the other passengers stood around us. She thought I hadn't seen her, that she was in 'stealth' mode, but I had clocked her. Nobody stood on that platform was above suspicion.

Short of going up and asking all the other passengers

what the nature or purpose of the journey was, I'm not sure what would have reassured her that we were not being followed.

There she stood in her best twinset and pearls, about to embark on an adventure to London to uncover the mystery that had consumed her entire life. How odd that it was the discovery of a mysterious bag of money on her beach that was the gateway to unlocking all of this.

As I allowed my mind to wander, a nagging worry tugged at me.

A complication she may have to grapple with and that I would have to support her through.

Once the investigator told her what he had discovered, should she make contact with William, assuming that was even possible? William might not even know he was adopted. If things had been as secretive and underhand as they appeared fifty years ago, many children were raised without ever knowing their true identity.

Was it even fair of Marjorie to enter his life now, if he didn't know? How would that affect his adopted family.

William would now be fifty years old. He could be a father, a grandfather. The implications for him are massive too.

I didn't think it would be enough for her to simply know the details of his life and walk away. She would want to meet him and hold him and tell him how, with all her heart, she'd loved him. But she would also need to consider the incredible impact that could have on him.

It would be a cruel irony if she were given details about her son but was unable to reach out to him. The best result of all would be that William was aware he was adopted and, better yet, that he was keen to meet her.

I wasn't going to allow my concerns to filter through to Marjorie. I put my doubts to one side and once Miss Marple was satisfied nobody was following us, we boarded the train. We walked confidently through the carriages until we found our seats in First Class. What an absolute treat.

We stowed our bags and jackets away as Marjorie got herself settled in, her handbag containing the loot

Only the Lonely

wrapped twice around her wrist.

When I returned from the bathroom, two glasses of chilled white wine sat on the table waiting. Despite it being only ten o'clock in the morning, we had finished them in no time and if by magic, they were replaced by two miniature bottles of pinot, along with two bags of salted peanuts.

Marjorie then pulled the itinerary from her handbag.

Of course there was an itinerary - this was Marjorie.

She smiled across at me brandishing a pen in case we needed to make adjustments or additions, but honestly, I was in awe of her plans:

Marjorie and Hetty travel to London

- Tuesday 17th May – 20th May 2022
- Tuesday 17th: First-class train from Truro, leave 10:00. Arrive 14:55 London Paddington
- Tuesday PM: Taxi to hotel.
- Tuesday Eve: Les Misérables, Queen's Theatre, West End
- Wednesday 18th AM: Visit Buckingham Palace & the Houses of Parliament
- Wednesday PM: Tate Modern, shopping/browsing on Oxford Street
- Wednesday 8.00pm: Dinner at Gordon Ramsay's Savoy Grill
- Thursday 19th AM: London Eye, walk through Hyde Park
- Thursday 1.00pm: Afternoon tea at The Ritz, shopping in Harrods
- Thursday 6.30pm: Dinner at Café Murano, Covent Garden
- Thursday 9.00pm: Cocktails at The American Bar at the Savoy
- Friday 20th 9.00am: Breakfast at Tiffany's, Harrods, Harry PI
- Friday: Train back to Truro

I looked across at Marjorie, now looking very pleased

with herself. I don't know what came over me, but I started to cry. Happy tears, but tears. Seeing me get upset, simply set Marjorie off too. How was this happening to us? How or why had fate sent that money to us? Us of all people. I know it was Marjorie that found it, but she was never going to keep it for herself. 'Money doesn't make people happy - sharing it does.'

I missed Albert too. I wished we'd been able to persuade him to join us, but I fear the sight of my new lace underwear had frightened him off.

We managed to pull ourselves together sipping the water the waitress brought us seeing our apparent distress.

"Wow, Marjorie, this itinerary is amazing, and of course, incredibly well organised. We're going to need a holiday after this trip; you do realise that don't you?"

"Well, Hetty, when are we going to get to come to London again? I've reserved all the big things, restaurants, the theatre, all thanks to Albert and online booking. The rest we can do as we feel. Is there anything you'd like to add, honey? I've totally taken over."

I don't know if it was the wine or the emotional breakdown I'd just recovered from, but I got a complete fit of the giggles and told her there was something very particular I wanted her to experience while we were away, but I'd leave it until we were out shopping to explain.

She looked at me, confused, then took a sip of her wine.

"I honestly don't know whether to be excited or worried, Hetty. You've got a very cheeky smile on your face and it's making me nervous."

"Ha, well it's nothing to be worried about, Marjorie. I just think it's something you need, and for once I hope you'll totally let yourself go. Look, stop looking so worried, pick up your wine. Cheers to us, my darling friend."

"Yes, cheers to us… but I'm still worried."

The rest of the journey proceeded without further revelations or tears. We managed two more bottles of pinot, a small selection of sandwiches and chocolate biscuits. When I say 'we', I mean 'I'. Marjorie sat quietly doing puzzles, gazing out of the window, and smiling at me as I devoured my picnic.

I checked my phone. Three text messages from each of my children, all wishing me the best time and reminding me to soak it up and make sure Marjorie had the time of her life. I replied to each of them but didn't mention it to Marjorie. I just prayed that one day it would be her texting her son or grandchildren.

I gazed out the window at the countryside rushing past and thought back to what it was like for her after William was taken. In the weeks that followed, her mother was cold and resentful towards her. Resentful to Majorie the nerve of the woman?

Marjorie had every right to feel resentment towards her.

I still feel angry about that, even now.

Thank goodness we got her out of that house when we did.

And now here she is, in possession of this mysterious sum of money. It could've come from anywhere - crime, or misfortune, who knows. Instead of fuelling something dark, it was financing joy. Helping a lifelong, law-abiding woman to find her son.

I think I dozed off after that, my head rocking gently against the window. Hopefully I didn't dribble. Marjorie didn't kick me, so I must've been alright.

The announcer told us the next stop was London Paddington. I got up to collect our coats. A woman who'd clearly seen our emotional start tapped me on the arm and wished us a wonderful trip, saying she hoped whatever had upset us would soon be resolved.

How kind was that? I thanked her thinking, if only you knew how much I wished that too.

We arrived and wheeled our cases up the ramp into the concourse. The first thing that struck us was the sheer volume of people.

Having lived in Cornwall all our lives, we were used to a slower pace. This was chaos. Everywhere were people with suitcases, briefcases, Starbucks cups and phones. Announcements rang out over the tannoy, whistles blew, train doors slammed.

Shops lined the station - food, clothes, newspapers,

cheap souvenirs. A Marks and Spencer, a florist, a shop full of Paddington Bear merchandise.

How people could live at this pace every day was beyond me. Maybe it was my advancing years, but at that moment, scanning the station for signs to the taxi rank, I did quietly yearn for Beachcombers. For the peace and quiet.

For a bench on a beach and the sounds of the sea.

CHAPTER TWENTY-SEVEN
Albert

I returned home from dropping my ladies at the train station to the most unbelievable surprise. As I pulled up outside my house, there, in my parking spot, was Emily. She jumped out of her car and rushed to me, throwing her arms around my neck. I was overjoyed.

We had spoken earlier in the week, and I had mentioned the ladies were off to London, but I hadn't expected her until the following day.

"I couldn't bear you being alone today Dad. I spoke to Hetty, who said what time you'd be back from the station. I added another day off work so I could surprise you."

She certainly had.

She was always such an incredibly thoughtful girl. I beamed at her as I ushered her inside. She fussed and flapped about me living in such a small home, but no amount of reassurance that it was just perfect for me seemed to put her mind at rest.

I had no need for a large house. It was too painful to consider the isolation of empty rooms with empty chairs and empty memories. I had the wealth to own such a property of course - a fact I had always hidden from my friends.

I was just happy to be here. I was painfully aware that my wealth might intimidate them and leave our financial positions unbalanced. I lived as frugally as the ladies did, but just as happily. We were equals in every sense, and I was glad of that. Money meant nothing to me. Having experienced such sadness with Kathleen, I sought happiness in the warmth offered by genuine, unencumbered friendship - and my precious daughter.

After a lunch of salmon and new potatoes with butter heaped on in amounts simply not allowed when Marjorie was around, we wrapped up and headed down to the beach. Emily linked her arm through mine as we chatted lightly and made each other laugh with silly stories.

She walked down to the water's edge, where she was joined by a rather playful cocker spaniel who dropped a stick at her feet, demanding she throw it again and again into the sea. The owners' shouts of "Lilly come here, I'm so sorry," went entirely unheard - I suspect by Emily as much as the dog.

She had longed for a dog when she was little, but our long working days had made it impractical. I sighed deeply as I watched her running along the beach with this random dog. She barked excitedly at her, waiting for the next throw. My heart swelled with so much love and pride for her.

Life had thrown two dreadful shocks her way, yet she had coped, and continued to cope, remarkably well.

Emily and I shared a love of movies, literature, and the arts. From a very young age she had an immensely inquisitive mind and loved a debate over dinner. It so reminded me of Kathleen and the discussions we had over suppers on our own or with the McBride's. She was, however, more of a lawyer than a medic and it was no surprise to me when she chose to study law at Newcastle University.

We both struggled when she elected to move so far away. We'd hoped she would choose to stay closer to home. When her university offers came through however, her mind was made up and she moved to the north-east to begin a journey into the law. She threw herself headlong into her studies and was clearly working towards earning a first.

Emily was so like me in many ways. She was driven to succeed, but as she approached her twenty-first birthday, she became very unwell. Her symptoms presented as fatigue, nausea, blood in her urine and severe back ache.

Only the Lonely

We advised her to visit her local GP immediately, but aware students seem to have different priorities, I wasn't convinced she would.

I was sufficiently concerned that I took time off work and drove up to Newcastle to see her for myself. Kathleen was annoyed at the time, thinking I was totally overreacting, but when she returned home that evening and I phoned to say that Emily was very ill, the bottom dropped out of our world.

I stayed in Newcastle at a local hotel overnight but arranged for her to be seen immediately at St George's Hospital back in London the following day.

My fear from looking at her, and from the symptoms she was exhibiting, was that Emily had a severe kidney infection, and I simply couldn't understand how she had been able to work as she was so ill. She underwent a series of blood tests and was referred to a renal specialist immediately, but all the indications pointed to a kidney failure.

Emily stayed at home with us until the results of her tests confirmed our worst fears. She was indeed in kidney failure and, sadly, it was sufficiently aggressive that we were advised that although treatment would start immediately, she may need a donor kidney.

Before we even left the consulting room, I was keen that they take samples of our blood to see if we were a compatible match for Emily. I was so shocked when Kathleen spoke up, saying surely it was too soon for our blood to be taken as the treatment might work.

I remember both Emily and I were looking at Kathleen, almost incredulous at her reticence at having the blood testing done. I agreed to it, of course. My precious girl needed her parents now more than ever.

Kathleen's reaction left me cold.

We hardly spoke on the journey home. She attempted to gloss over her reaction saying it was simply nerves about needles, but it just didn't sit well with me, and goodness knows what Emily made of it. Kathleen had had plenty of needles whilst we were trying for Emily and had never indicated nerves about them. I couldn't help but think there was something more behind it, but I just couldn't see what. Or wouldn't allow myself to.

I knew Emily had picked up on her mother's reticence to have the blood tests, which made it all the more difficult to understand. It was true that Kathleen had quickly changed her attitude and provided the sample, but it was her initial reaction that I was struggling to make sense of.

What I couldn't quite understand was that the surgeon had made it clear there was a chance Emily would respond well to treatment and that a donor kidney might not even be necessary. The blood tests were worth doing now so that, if the time came, we would already know whether either of us was a suitable match.

I waited until Emily had taken herself out for a walk before supper to raise it with Kathleen.

"What was that about at the clinic, Kathleen? Please don't say you've no idea what I mean, we both know what I'm referring to. Emily even picked up on it."

Kathleen was a calm, gentle woman. She was not given to open displays of anger or emotional outbursts, which I had long put down to her legal training and the need to remain composed with clients and adversaries. But she rounded on me.

"Just leave it Albert, just leave it. Why do you always have to be the perfect parent who reacts exactly how a perfect parent should? I was just in shock, alright? I'm not a doctor. I was hoping you were wrong, and that Em would be fine, but she's not fine, this is not fine, nothing about this is fine.

For once in your life stop being a robot and understand that people react to this kind of news differently. There's no right or wrong way to react to something like that, is there?"

Before I could even reply, she grabbed her laptop and phone and left the kitchen. I heard her slam the door to her study, and I understood that the conversation was well and truly over. This was clearly an issue she was not prepared to explore further.

Her reaction, however, only raised more concerns in me. We had been married just short of twenty-five years, and I had never seen her behave, or react, like this.

I slumped into my chair, stunned and hurt that this was how she really viewed me. Was I truly the caricature of the perfect parent? Was I so emotionally blinkered that I couldn't accept that people react differently? I honestly didn't think so.

But this wasn't and shouldn't be about us. Right now, our daughter needed the unity and strength of her parents. I couldn't quite square what was happening in Kathleen's mind, but I wasn't prepared to add to Emily's anxiety by letting her see us feuding.

I left it twenty minutes, then knocked on her study door and walked in. Kathleen had clearly been crying but was sitting with her laptop open, apparently working.

"Look, Kathleen, I'm sorry if I spoke out of turn. You're quite right, we do all react differently to devastating news, and I shouldn't assume my reaction will be yours.

I'm going to make supper now. Why don't you run yourself a bath? I'll bring you up a glass of wine. Emily doesn't need to see us falling out, not on top of everything else she's trying to process today."

Kathleen got up from behind her desk and put her arms around my neck.

"I'm sorry too, Albert. You will never know how incredibly sorry I am."

I felt something shift as she looked at me.

I saw something new and troubling.

It had a name, but I couldn't speak it.

It left me so uneasy.

It was guilt.

CHAPTER TWENTY-EIGHT
Marjorie

We managed to navigate our way through the train station to the taxi rank, our newly purchased wheeled suitcases proving to be a godsend, making life considerably easier.

I asked the driver to take us to The Savoy with what I hoped was a quiet air of confidence, as if being driven to that establishment, was an everyday occurrence. However, I was with Hetty, who just blurted it out so that everyone in the queue heard our destination anyway.

Our driver was a simply delightful man. Instead of heading straight to the hotel, he took us via Kensington and Knightsbridge. We even passed Harrods, where I would be meeting my investigator to hear what I prayed would be the news that could make my life complete.

As we pulled up outside the hotel, two doormen dressed in heavy navy coats with gold buttons came over to the taxi. One of them opened the door and held out his hand to help us out, whilst the other went to the other side and took our bags, placing them neatly onto a gold trolley.

"Good afternoon, ladies, and welcome to The Savoy."

I felt like royalty. I paid and tipped our taxi driver with cash - something I knew I would have to become more accustomed to spending.

Hetty was standing holding the driver's hand. She wished him the very best for his wife, who had been ill for several weeks - the doctors still unsure of the problem. She also hoped his little girl settled in at nursery and reassured him that some children just took a little longer, but she was sure she would be fine.

This was, no doubt, an indication of how the trip was going to be - Hetty constantly learning the life story of total strangers.

The hotel was breath-taking. The reception area was stunning, with large chequerboard tiles and the most beautiful flower arrangements. The aromas were a rich mixture of gardenia and jasmine infused with lemon scents from neroli oils.

The staff couldn't have been more helpful or welcoming. Our rooms were ready, and they happily checked us in and carried our bags across the concourse to the lift.

Hetty's face as the bellboy opened the door to her room was priceless. The views across the river were spectacular and looked exactly as they had in the literature. I had no doubts the rooms would be amazing - they did not disappoint.

Hetty immediately sat on her bed and lay back with her feet dangling off the floor. She asked the young man showing us around where the dressing gown was, and if he knew how much they cost. He laughed at her excitement and showed us the gowns and slippers hanging in the wardrobe. He also pointed out the room service and extras guide, should we wish to purchase anything.

He then enquired whether we would like the turn-down service for later that evening. We both looked at each other, totally confused by what that might mean. I could see Hetty working herself up to a cheeky response.

"Do we look like we ever get turned down? Look at us - we're gorgeous!"

He blushed and laughed putting his arm across his mouth. He explained that, when we returned later, our beds would be made ready with the top sheet folded back and a chocolate placed on the pillow – this was known as the 'turn-down' service.

How marvellous. We both agreed that was the kind of 'turn-down' we would thoroughly enjoy, thank you very much.

I tipped him handsomely (I'd done my research) and told

him he didn't need to show me to my room, as it was just next door and no doubt identical to Hetty's.

I sprayed on generous amounts of perfume and knocked on Hetty's unlocked door. She wasn't ready, of course, and her room already looked like the stalls at a bring-and-buy sale. I busied myself picking up dresses, trousers, shoes and underwear. I knew she had large breasts, but seeing one of Hetty's bras outside of breasts was a truly serious undertaking.

She came out of the bathroom, still putting an earring in. She looked stunning.

"My goodness, Hetty, you look amazing. I love that dress. Burnt orange is so your colour!"

"Ah, thanks Marj, you look lovely yourself. Here we are, Thelma and Louise on the adventure of a lifetime and looking fabulous. Cornwall on Tour!"

We went back downstairs, and a taxi was hailed to take us to the Queen's Theatre for our first treat - Les Misérables. Too early for the show, we made our way to a nearby wine bar. A swanky venue with a wonderful hum of chatter, cutlery on china plates and the clinking of glasses. We ordered two glasses of fizz as we read the menu.

As we were enjoying the last of our cream tea, a taste of home we couldn't resist, we were alerted to an angry exchange at a table across from us.

A woman in her thirties, wearing unfeasibly high heels and more lipstick than I would apply in a month, marched up to a table occupied by four other women. She scanned their faces and, in a tone far too sharp for such an upmarket venue, asked,

"Which one of you is Phee?"

Three of the women turned to look at a rather beautiful blonde lady. Her tan belied the dull weather London had been experiencing, and the dress she was squeezed into, might have looked better on someone who actually was a size ten. (I'm merely saying what I know Hetty was also clearly thinking).

She looked up from her large gin and tonic, and with an incredibly fake smile, replied,

"I'm sorry, do I know you?"

"Well, no, you don't actually, Phee. But I wonder if you would care to explain why, when I was having sex with my husband last night, he whispered your name into my ear? One quick search of his Instagram friends and 'boom' there you were."

I had to kick Hetty under the table.

Her mouth was agape, spoon hanging limp from her fingers.

I signalled to the waiter to bring our bill, while the silence at the next table was deafening. Then, after a pause, the woman continued,

"Well, Phee? Wanna explain that to me?"

The head waiter - whom I now know is called the maître d'- had been summoned and charged over to their table.

"Is everything okay here, ladies? There's no problem, is there?"

Our original waiter returned with the bill and a card machine, but I told him I would be paying with cash. He assured me that was fine and invited me to leave it in the narrow bill folder.

As I reached for my handbag, (I had it looped around my ankle, just in case) the woman I now knew to be Phee stood up, grabbed her coat and bag, and stormed out. This left 'too-much-lipstick lady' looming over the table.

"You lot tell that sly bitch to stay away from my husband - or next time, it won't just be a quiet word over dinner."

She then turned to the waiter.

"No, I'm sorry, Anthony. Everything's fine. There's no problem now - the problem just left."

I left the payment and a tip (I was getting more confident with that), and as we stepped outside into the cool May air. I looked at Hetty and we both burst out laughing.

"Bloody hell, Marjorie. You bring me to London for culture and top-class dining, and we end up on the set of a soap opera! You wouldn't get that happening at Penny's Pastries and Puddings in Padstow, would you? Dirty old Phee, eh? She didn't even deny it!"

We were still wrapped in laughter when 'too-much-lipstick lady' came outside too. She looked at us as we tried to compose ourselves, trying not to look like naughty schoolgirls.

"Thought I handled that quite well, don't you, ladies?"

We agreed she had.

She lit a cigarette and made her way towards Covent Garden.

"I think I'm going to enjoy our trip, Hetty."

"I already am, Marjorie. I already am."

CHAPTER TWENTY-NINE
Hetty

Getting into the swing of things in London, we walked out into the road to hail a taxi from outside the Theatre. What a most fantastic night watching Les Misérables. I'm not convinced I quite understand what it was about, but the music and costumes were incredible. Ironic that we should watch a play about war given what preceded it in the wine bar.

I wouldn't say I enjoyed watching people argue, but I have to admit, it was most amusing. The look of shock on Marjorie's face made it all worthwhile. I was surprised she didn't march over and remind her that shouting was most unbecoming of a lady - even if her husband had been caught cheating.

In spite of everything she'd been through, Michael leaving her, William being taken, and then resigning herself to a life that was emotionally and romantically alone, Marjorie remained, outwardly at least, a tower of strength. She has always been my dearest friend.

When I was attacked for the final time by Edwin, Marjorie was once again my rock - as were my children. I stayed in hospital for five days so severe were my injuries. Marjorie visited me daily, which was a source of great comfort.

Although my physical scars were healing well, the emotional toll of watching Edwin self-destruct was much harder to bear.

My children saw things in black and white - I should leave him. I understood that. In spite of everything, I couldn't shake myself free of loving him. When I said 'I do' all those years ago, it meant something. It still did. Broken cheekbone or not, Edwin was my husband.

That loyalty ended however, the night I sat alone, on a white plastic chair, in a hospital side room, being told my husband had finally crossed the line and had taken another man's life.

Edwin had gone into Newquay drinking and had started a fight with a man in a pub. He broke a glass and slashed the man across the face. The man had to be rushed to hospital for emergency surgery.

Before emergency services even arrived, Edwin fled the pub. As two women were getting into their car after collecting a takeaway, he stole their vehicle and sped off.

Shortly after, on the A3059 between Newquay and Trellinick, he crashed into another vehicle. The car he hit had rolled into a ditch and was later found by a passing motorist.

Edwin had to be cut free from the wreckage and was in critical condition - the same hospital I had been discharged from just two days earlier.

I was numb.

The doctors explained that although Edwin was currently unconscious from head injuries, they could arrange a visit if I wished.

Without hesitation, I told them I did not.

'Life has a way of sorting things out.'

It may take time, it may take heartache, or even the kindness, or the stupidity of others, but things will eventually sort themselves out. That was a mantra often trotted out by my darling mother.

But as I sat there, shaking and cold, listening to the catalogue of crimes my wretched husband had committed, I realised the prophetic truth of that statement.

At a terrible price, had he just granted me and my children peace.

If Edwin pulled through, it would not matter which barrister represented him, they would struggle to explain or justify what Edwin had done.

But his biggest struggle would not be a legal one.

Before any judge or jury could pass judgement on him, he finally did the last remaining decent thing open to him.

He died.

Blameless.

Alone.

I allowed my memories to creep back into their box and turned back to Marjorie. She was surreptitiously counting out the taxi fee from inside her handbag. Her paranoia, though slightly less obvious, was clearly still cloying at her. Before leaving the hotel, she'd put the investigators money and the bulk of the spending money in the safe. We'd agreed that we would only take out an amount needed for 'a bloody good time.'

With the end of our first night approaching, I felt confident that a good time would indeed be on the cards for this trip. I'd make sure of it.

Not just for me. But for incredible woman sat opposite me in a taxi, in London, counting money in a handbag, the origins of which we had no clue, on our way back to the Savoy after watching Les Misérables.

Unbelievable.

But true.

CHAPTER THIRTY
Albert

I had received seven texts from Marjorie and twelve from Hetty. Hetty's messages also included photographs; bottles of wine, smiling faces, outside the theatre and their hotel rooms. Thankfully I do not need a pacemaker as she also sent me one of her in the underwear I'd taken delivery of for her.

My poor heart.

Thankfully Emily was not sat with me when I opened that one – goodness knows what she'd have thought. I deleted it immediately.

I was thrilled they had arrived safely and were clearly not holding back on enjoying themselves. I'm sure like them, I would not fully relax into the trip until they met with Harry and discovered what he'd uncovered about William. He'd needed a few extra days so that meant it would have to be the last thing on Marjorie's extensive itinerary.

I supposed the anticipation would be awful. Although that seemed an impossibly difficult wait for them both, if Harry's investigations were ultimately not the outcome Marjorie hoped for, the whole trip would be ruined if it was the first thing on their list of things to do. Better it was the last thing.

I remained sat on Marjorie's bench whilst Emily, now no longer playing with her doggy friend, wandered down across the shoreline, gather netting and other bits of beach detritus she regarded as potentially harmful to animals.

I was so blessed to have her in my life. My constant.

I was at the surgery when I got the call from Emily's consultant, James Winterbourne. I'd known James for a great many years and, ironically, he had watched Emily grow as our children had attended the same school. He asked if it were possible for me to come and see him, and not to mention it to Kathleen at this stage as there was just something he wanted to chat to me about.

I obviously went cold.

Had there been more bad news from Emily's latest scan or set of bloods? I honestly couldn't bear the thought that she was worse than we initially thought. I cleared my schedule for the afternoon and drove across to the hospital to see him.

It was the worst kind of eight-mile journey where I battled not telling Kathleen. It seemed disloyal to not tell her where I was going. James had been clear, don't tell Kathleen at this stage.

The walk through the hospital corridors with the rapid pounding in my heart left me in danger of passing out and in need of a doctor myself. As I reached the renal ward, I let James's secretary know I was there to see him, took a seat and allowed my heartbeat to slow.

As a doctor myself, there's a certain face I have in reserve for delivering bad or difficult news to a patient. It was clear James utilised the same technique. He came to his office door with a face that told me to brace myself. I stood and walked into his room. We shook hands and he offered me a seat and a coffee. I declined the coffee but accepted the water he was pouring into two glasses. He had an anonymous file on his side of the desk, which he opened as he sat down.

'Albert, I just wanted to talk to you myself, you know, alone. This isn't about Emily exactly her blood work was fine. Look, there's no easy to tell you this mate, there's a problem with your blood results."

My head at this point was a whirl. I hated the soft tone in his voice; I sensed that bad news was coming.

"Let me tell you about our processes again. I know this is probably all stuff you know but bear with me. As possible donors we analyse your bloods for DNA matches as well as blood types. Sorry if I'm stating the obvious here mate, I know you know the drill, but those are the stages we go through, first blood group, then DNA match. Here's where we hit a problem, Albert."

The confusion and pain on my face must have been obvious to him as he stood up and came and sat in the chair next to mine. The walls of the room were closing in and there was a screaming in my head. My heart was pounding so hard at my chest, I honestly thought I would be sick.

"What are you saying, James, what did the DNA tell you?"

"You are not Emily's father, Albert. I am so very sorry. I had the sample re-tested in case it was wrong, but the same results were returned. Emily and Kathleen matched, but you didn't."

When you hear news that is just so outside your comprehension, that you are just too ill-prepared for, what takes over is a primeval need for a corner. A need to be held firm by a solid wall away from everyone and everything.

A corner of a wall that you can slide down and curl up against the news and clutch on to yourself and hide. Where you can scream and say you're wrong, that you've made a mistake, because these kinds of things don't happen to me.

I kept my head down, my hands in balls against my knees as James put his hand on my shoulder and squeezed.

"Albert I am so bloody sorry. It's totally shit. There's no other way to describe it. I actually feel sick, telling you. This was why I didn't want Kathleen here today. I wanted you to know first so you can decide how you would like to proceed. Let me get you some tea, Albert, you need something warm."

I didn't want something warm. I wanted my wife. I wanted answers.

I stayed with James for over an hour, and he showed me the DNA profiles and how they were able to confirm I was not Emily's father. I was honestly stunned. Never in all of Em's twenty years had I ever questioned whether she was mine, it had never even entered my head.

Why would it? The joy Kathleen and I felt when she became pregnant after years of trying never once gave rise to suspicions. Yes we'd struggled for her to conceive, but I just thought we'd finally struck lucky. After years of trying, the planets aligned, and we made a baby.

Now what was I supposed to do?

This didn't alter the facts of Emily's illness. She didn't need this shock on top of everything she was dealing with. I probably should say nothing to her at least. But then I feared how I would be with Kathleen when I returned home.

Should I not just confront her outright and ask who the father was? Should I just continue as if today hadn't happened and hope with every bone in my body that Em continued to do well, and the issue of transplant was never required?

I could wait to see if we ever reached the point of needing a transplant and then confront her as it would be necessary to ask the real father to be a possible donor. Oh my god, this was all just such a mess. How was this even happening?

I left James's room with the file and the heaviest of hearts. My world had just been turned upside down. Not only had I just learnt that the love of my life had been unfaithful to me but had done so at a time when we were trying for a baby of our own. Becoming pregnant by her lover was always a risk. Clearly.

My precious daughter Emily. I still loved her the same now, with this news, as I did before I entered James's room. How was I ever going to make sense of the fact that she actually had a father out there who was unknown to both Emily and I. Ironically, a secret that now binds us, even though she is totally unaware of it. Of course, this would explain Kathleen's reluctance to have our bloods analysed. She would have been carrying this possibility all of Emily's life.

I sat back in my car at the hospital feeling more alone than I had ever felt in my life. I put the file on the passenger seat and as I did, tears started to roll down my cheeks. How was I supposed to drive home and pretend

this hadn't happened and be myself around Kathleen?
I needed to drive the long way home and think.
Should I say something?
Or should I quietly hold onto this – potentially forever?

CHAPTER THIRTY-ONE
Marjorie

The whole experience of being at a West End show had excited us both. Hetty had commented as we made the short walk from the wine bar to the theatre, that we had already seen a little drama play out earlier and if this play were half as thrilling she would be happy! I still hadn't gotten over that by the way. Naughty old Phee. Fancy being caught out at in front of friends.

"You don't think that was all a ploy to distract us do you Hetty? Whilst we were watching that minidrama play out, you don't think anyone planted tracking devices in our coats or on our handbags do you? I'm still a nervous wreck about this money. What if someone followed us to London?'

"Marjorie what the heck are you talking about. That Phee was just caught red handed. Other than the waiting on staff, nobody came near our table anyway. Stop worrying. Honestly what are you like?!"

"Yes, you're probably right honey, I should just relax. What an exciting few days we've got ahead of us.'

When we arrived at the theatre, we ordered wine and worked out by watching everyone else that we could order another glass to have during the interval, which Hetty was thrilled about. The lady explained that when we came downstairs during the break, our drinks would be on the counter with our seat numbers under the glass. How terribly efficient and I pointed that out to her and gave her a tip.

Hetty was still behaving like an excited schoolgirl on a trip, but I loved that about her. She eyed the other theatregoers up and down and graded them on what they were wearing. 'Wouldn't be seen dead in that,' or 'Her dress is to die for, Marjorie, look!' Her fashion analysis was forensic, if a little harsh at times. That's not to say I hadn't been a little judgy myself in the wine bar!

As Hetty reviewed outfits, I was eyeing the scene for anyone looking at us or talking into hidden microphones in jacket lapels. I'd seen that in lots of crime shows and films so it must go on in real life. I observed no such behaviour thankfully, so I allowed myself to relax.

I managed to purchase two programmes and Hetty tried to make intelligent conversation about the plot from sections she was reading, "Ooh, I hadn't realised he was in Casualty before this?" She went on, "Did you know Marjorie, this story was actually written by Victor Hugo and is a crime thriller about prostitution and theft and escaping from the law?"

The performance was perfection. The songs stirring and the theatre sets, quite unlike anything I had ever seen before. We were late arriving back to our hotel so just decided to retire immediately, with a day of sight-seeing and shopping planned for the following day. We arranged to meet for breakfast at 9.30. We kissed each other on the cheek as Hetty burst into a rendition of 'I Dreamed a Dream' and disappeared into her turned-down room for our first night at The Savoy.

As I walked into my room, I too was greeted by turned-down sheets and a cute chocolate on my pillow. My slippers were ready for me by my bed, and I thought I bet Hetty is beside herself, as the dressing gown was laid out ready to be used. I undressed and showered before climbing into the biggest bed I had ever been in. I lay still, taking in the room and wondering how on earth this was happening.

Was I really at The Savoy? Did I really just watch Les Mis and why was I the one to find that windfall? I was snapped out of my thoughts by my phone ringing, and I had no doubts about who it would be.

"How amazing is the room, Marjorie? Did you have a chocolate on your pillow, have you walked around in your dressing gown yet? I am, right now, totally in the buff but for my dressing gown, and where is Jean

Valjean when you need him?"

"Ha ha, well if he saw that, Hetty, he'd be on the run again! Go to sleep, you mad woman, we have a busy day again tomorrow. I love you, Hetty. Au revoir!"

"Yeah, he would be on the run again, straight into this bed for a bit of Cornish hospitality! Night, Marjorie, I love you too and thank you so much for this trip, I'm loving every second."

I rose typically early and went for a walk around the hotel and outside along the Thames for some fresh air before joining Hetty at 9.30 in the Savoy Grill as planned for breakfast. She had already taken a seat and as I walked in was ordering English breakfast tea for herself and a lemon tea for me (she knows me so well).

"Well, Hetty how did you sleep in your luxury bed big enough for six people?"

"Like a baby once I finally dropped off. My mind was a whirl of yesterday's goings-on and excitement for today's."

The plan for today was to see Buckingham Palace, a walk up The Mall, along to the Houses of Parliament and then the Tate Modern and shopping. I knew Hetty wasn't too keen on the idea of the Tate, so I decided to play that one by ear.

"Now, Hetty, you mentioned on the train there was something you had in mind you wanted me to 'experience' while we were in London and I don't want you thinking I'm being too bossy, dragging you everywhere I want to go. Would this afternoon be a suitable time for that?'

"Well, yes and no, it's a purchase I would like us both to make today but 'experience' tonight. I'm going to take you to Ann Summers, Marjorie. This treat is on me."

"Ann Summers, who's she?"

"She's not a who, it's a shop and a very specific one at that."

"Ooh, that sounds lovely, Hetty. Hang on. I've brought my itinerary with me; I'll add Ann Summers on to this afternoon. What does she sell in her shop?"

"Do you know what, Marjorie, I'm going to leave that as a surprise for later today. Let's enjoy our breakfast and then I'm going to put my trainers on, and we'll take a walk like the royalty we are, down The Mall. Just one thing though, Marj, just a bit of fun over breakfast while it's just us girls - if you could spend the night in that enormous bed upstairs with any man, who would it be?"

Majorie looked up from her eggs benedict with shock on her face.

"My goodness, Hetty, we're having breakfast at The Savoy, where on earth did that come from?"

"Never mind that, I just need to know for later. Who would you choose?"

"For later, what does that even mean?"

"Marjorie, honestly, just trust me, who makes your heart flutter when they're on TV? Pick anyone you like. I'll help you. As you well know, I'm crazy about Colin Firth. What I wouldn't give to show Colin around my en-suite facilities."

Marjorie hid her giggles behind her serviette as she struggled to think of a name to such and outrageous question.

"Well, honestly, Hetty, thank goodness nobody is sat by us. What a conversation to be having whilst using solid silver cutlery. Alan Titchmarsh. That's who I would choose, the lovely Alan Titchmarsh. Though frankly, we'd probably just sit up in that super king-sized bed all night talking about plants, tubs or borders. He's a wonderful gardener. So good with his hands.

No, don't say what I know you're itching to say, Hetty, that's just too rude!"

"Alan Titchmarsh … Haha, well fair enough, Marj, it's your choice - so Alan it is."

"I've no idea what you're plotting, Hetty, but you've certainly made me nervous. As if I'm not on edge enough."

We set off for our walk to Buckingham Palace. Hetty couldn't resist purchasing a ridiculous 'I heart London' hat from a stall holder, making us both look like American tourists which, while not meant as an insult to

American tourists, was not an accurate portrayal of who we were.

She took so many pictures of herself, invariably dragging me into them, which she then sent to Albert and no doubt forwarded to her children too. She had set my phone up with the new WhatsApp app for this trip and, I have to say, I loved it. You can set up groups for whatever you like and just invite who you want to view your texts and pictures. This group was called London2022 and just the three of us were members.

I was able to view Albert's adorable replies to the photographs, and he was able to send us photographs of him watering my tubs and sweeping the leaves off our paths. He is just so thoughtful. London or no London, he knew I wouldn't be able to rest if I thought there was a build-up of leaves on the path to my front door.

He was even wearing the navy woollen jumper and the beloved red scarf we bought him for his birthday last year in the Harbour Store in Padstow. It made me miss him. Though we were both delighted to see Emily had come to keep him company, we'd have preferred to have him with us.

Hetty let me read her text to him that it was like being with Miss Marple in London as I was just so paranoid. "Well," I said, "It's a jolly good job I am on my toes. We have a great deal of illicit cash with us, and the intended owner may just want it back."

I looked across at Hetty, who was trying to persuade a Metropolitan Police Officer with a rather menacing-looking machine gun to have a picture with her. He declined but pointed her to a Community Police Officer who was considerably more amenable to this nutty Cornish/American tourist. I loved the innocent fun in her. For all she had been through with Edwin, she still managed to find the fun and joyous side to life.

After a light lunch of Welsh rarebit (posh cheese on toast), tea and a fresh cream strawberry tart, we set off to Ann Summers. Hetty giggled every time she looked at me on the way there, which simply made me increasingly nervous. Once we arrived outside the shop, I understood why.

"You must be kidding me, Hetty. There's simply no way I'm going in there. Is it a sex shop?"

"No come on, Marj, it's not a sex shop, I promise you. It's a sexy shop, that's different."

"No way Hetty, sexy or otherwise, what would I be doing in a shop like this and what if somebody sees us?"

"Well, you know what, Marjorie, lots of people are going to see us but here's the important thing, none of them know us. So, who cares? You said this trip would be a journey into the unknown, well I intend for you to have exactly that tonight so come on, stop being so silly. Open your mind up to new experiences, Marjorie, and let yourself go. Audrey Hepburn would have been right up for this store, I promise you, she was a girl game for some fun. Park Marjorie for a bit, relax and let's have some fun in here, Marj. I know exactly what we're getting - you're not the only one to have done some research."

We entered the store, and it really was like stepping into a nightmare, a very sexy, inappropriate nightmare. Everywhere I looked there were mannequins wearing underwear with frankly no discernible purpose other than to highlight the versatility of red ribbon on black knickers and bras (such as you could call them knickers and bras). They certainly offered no support or warmth.

The shop was awash with either young women or young couples and as a result, Hetty and I stood out like sore thumbs.

I didn't want to ruin Hetty's surprise, whatever that was going to be, so I decided to try and play it cool, like I was fine about being in there. I started to look at the various displays and merchandise. I honestly couldn't work out what most of the equipment was for, where it would go or what you would do with it. I decided to stick with Hetty, who was marching on with great purpose deeper into the store.

I was mortified when I saw her approach a member of staff who was hanging handcuffs with various coloured feathers onto a display. Handcuffs? What would you do with them and why feathers?

"Where would I find vibrators, please?"

Only the Lonely

The lady stopped what she was doing and pointed us over to a large display area on the righthand side of the shop, "They're over there, give me a shout if you need any help with anything ladies, it's a bit of a minefield."

Hetty confidently replied, 'Thanks, honey, that's great. I think I know what we're after, but I'll seek you out if we can't find them. Come on, Missy, time to get you sorted for tonight."

"What with, Hetty? What is a vibrator?"

"Come on and I'll show you. Meredith from book club has one of these, Marjorie, she told me at dinner the other night. She was not even bothered that Olive and Norman were listening too. She said it makes her toes curl, it's that good. So, I thought to myself, while we're here in London and nobody knows us, why don't we get some toe-curling done for once."

"What does that even mean, Hetty. Do I want my toes curled?"

"Well from what Meredith said to me, yes, we both bloody do. Here they are. Let me grab two of those. Now is there anything else that's caught your eye, Marj?"

"You're kidding me, right? What the heck are those, Hetty, what do you do with them?"

"Let me go and pay for them, then when we get outside, I'll explain what you do."

"Just these please, we are buying them for our friends."

"Would your friends like lube with these, ladies?"

Hetty looked at me with a blank expression and I had to hope she wasn't looking for clarification as I had no idea what that was either. She turned back to the lady and simply said "No, I think they'll be fine without the lube, thank you."

I offered to give Hetty some windfall cash, but she insisted on paying with her card. Now everyone at the bank would know she had shopped with Ann Summers - the embarrassment of it all.

We got outside and Hetty immediately took her phone out and typed 'lube' into Google. She read the first description that came up and then said, "Sorry, Marj, turns out we probably do need lube, we need to go back in for a second."

We promptly went back inside and Hetty said to the same lady, still standing behind the till, "Sorry, I just checked with our friends, and it turns out they do want lube after all."

She smiled at us both, not unkindly, then put two tubes of what looked like toothpaste in our original bags. We paid and left.

Thank goodness there wasn't a raid on the shop whilst we were in there. Imagine us being on Crimewatch CCTV footage. If poor Albert were watching that he'd faint if he saw us in a sexy shop buying sex toys.

To be fair to Hetty that shop certainly was an experience. Once outside she suggested we take a break and find somewhere to have coffee. She would run through what was what. I hid the Ann Summers bags in my larger bag. I obviously wasn't going to allow her to take one of them out in the street and we certainly needed a coffee shop that afforded us some privacy.

If I'm honest, I was secretly curious about having my toes curled.

We found a little corner seat in a cute coffee shop just off Oxford Street, ordered two cappuccinos and sat down. I couldn't quite believe I was ordering cappuccinos these days. My choice of beverages would typically only extend to English breakfast tea or lemon tea. But here I was in London, and I had just been in a sex toy shop, so a cappuccino seemed positively humdrum by comparison.

Once our coffees arrived, Hetty once again brought up Google and searched, let's say, some 'educational' pages which we read together trying not to draw attention to our uncontrolled laughter. I was relieved we would not be researching this on the hotels Wi-Fi. I'm not going to be graphic here, but let's just say I learnt things about my own body I was not previously aware of.

"Okay, Marj, so armed with this new information, I want you to take your toy, who is now renamed Alan Titchmarsh, and go off to your enormous bed tonight and have some fun. I hope Colin Firth and I have a night neither of us will ever forget. Christ it's been so long."

We burst into fits of laughter and the Marks and Spencer four-pack of knickers proved very useful. Hetty really does have a weak pelvic floor! I had to hope our latest purchases wouldn't make it worse.

We finished our coffees, 'freshened up', then set off down Oxford Street to take in more of the shops and sights and sounds of central London. (It's probably obvious that we didn't make it to the Tate Modern, but in a sense that was made up for by the two pieces of golden sculpture we were bringing back to the hotel. I just hoped the wonderfully friendly doormen didn't enquire about our purchases).

What a long day. We both felt exhausted. We went back to my room, sat up on the bed and put Pointless on the TV. I do enjoy this show and the genuine friendship that clearly exists between Alexander Armstrong and Richard Osman. I imagine them to be great pals that go off to the pub and the football together or share interesting facts about history or literature with one another.

However, no sooner had the show started, we both fell sound asleep, Hetty's head nestled perfectly into my neck. We woke at seven just as the music for The One Show was starting. Hetty went back to her room, and we agreed to meet at 7.45 for a cheeky drink before our evening rendezvous at the inhouse Gordon Ramsey restaurant at the Savoy Grill.

I had bought a sequined royal blue dress with a silver pashmina, silver shoes and handbag. I didn't anticipate Gordon actually being there, but one simply never knows. I was ready quite quickly, so I took my 'item' out of the packaging, plugged the USB into the wall socket and pressed the button on the front. It immediately started vibrating, making a buzzing sound. 'Well Alan, where am I going to hide you while I wait for my turn-down service?' I left it plugged in until I heard Hetty tap on the door. Again, she looked amazing in a little black dress with a cream jacket and shoes. Very classy.

"Come in, Hetty, have you plugged Colin in?"

"Yes, he's on charge. I need a full charge for what I want from him later."

"Hetty you can't, what about your turndown service?"

"I've turned it down, Marj, the lady is in the corridor now, do you want me to tell her to leave your room too?"

"Oh yes, go on then, save me hiding it. God I'm mortified, Hetty. If anyone ever finds out about this I would die of embarrassment."

Hetty lent into the corridor and told the lady my room did not require the turn-down service either.

"Right, I told her, so she knows. Stop worrying. What happens in London, stays in

London."

"Well, if my investigator has found my William I wouldn't want him knowing his mother was up to all sorts in London. No, this stays between us and doesn't make the journey back to Trellinick. Sorry Hetty."

"Fair enough"! Now Ms Hepburn, are you ready to dine with Gordon Ramsey?'

We went down to the restaurant and had the most amazing meal and far too much wine, but the ambience and evening warranted it. Our feet were throbbing in our tight-fitting heels and increasingly as the evening progressed they spent more time off our feet than on. The staff were fussing over us like we were celebrities, and nothing was too much trouble. The fish was cooked to perfection, and I can honestly say that I have never tasted such a beautiful dessert in my life. A chocolate and avocado mousse which was simply divine. Who would have thought avocado would go with chocolate? I would definitely be making that at supper club on our return.

Hetty opted for the cheese board, which again was simply unbelievable and which I was more than happy to help her with. When the meal ended, we were both squiffy and very giggly and had become best friends with both the wine waiter and the restaurant manager, who took a particular interest in ensuring our night was perfect, which it was.

We took the lift back to our rooms and both giggled

uncontrollably at the prospect of what lay ahead. As we got to my door, Hetty said,

"Have the best night, Marjorie Hepburn. Just let yourself go and enjoy. I bloody intend too. I'm here, Colin, have you been waiting long?"

CHAPTER THIRTY-TWO
Hetty

We met at the restaurant for breakfast at 9.30, as we had the previous day. I sat down opposite Marjorie who looked up from her menu, a playful grin on her face.

"Well, good morning, Marjorie."

"Good morning, Hetty. Did you sleep well?"

"Eventually yes. But only after some serious toe curling!"

"Me too"

"Blimey, Hetty. Who knew?"

"I know right. I'm exhausted. Colin Firth is enjoying a lie-in this morning."

"I haven't even seen Alan this morning."

Two tired celebrities.

Two elated tourists.

CHAPTER THIRTY-THREE
Albert

Emily walked back up the beach, beach debris in hand, and sat next to me on Marjorie's bench. I recounted, probably not for the first time, how Marjorie would sit here every day and enjoy her tea. She humoured me and allowed me to talk. She probably sensed I was missing my two companions so talking about them was a comfort - which it was.

Throughout everything I had gone through with Kathleen, Emily had remained so stoic. At the worst of times, she was the only positive, the only dependable person in my life.

Yet I knew that was unfair. I could not, and should not, lean on my daughter like that. I was a grown man. I had to work this out without relying on Emily for strength. But what I simply couldn't fathom was that Kathleen had carried a lie this enormous for so long. That she had become pregnant and kept the truth hidden until she was forced, by Emily's illness, to come clean.

I have replayed that confrontation so many times. After hearing such devastating news, I was left to process a new kind of life. One where I would remain a dad but was no longer Emily's biological father.

The journey home from the hospital took almost three hours, a combination of rush-hour traffic and a stop at Starbucks. I chose to drink my coffee in the café, hoping the time might help me absorb what I had just been told.

Emily was not my daughter.

I hated thinking that. Of course she was still my daughter. But now that truth would forever be challenged by biology. I couldn't believe Kathleen had been so duplicitous. I had given her my whole life. I had loved her with all my heart and had never once doubted her.

I remembered reading a Kurt Vonnegut book, Mother Night, where he said, "We are what we pretend to be, so we must be careful about what we pretend to be."

Kathleen had been careful. She had pretended to be a loyal wife and loving mother. But she had slept with someone else. She had hidden from both Emily and I that my daughter might not be mine. It's possible she had known for years. With her access to legal forensic labs, it would have been easy to test a few hairs strands.

If she had known, and kept that secret from me, then it was a terrible cruelty.

I looked up at the other coffee drinkers, chatting over lattes, whilst children smeared chocolate over their faces. How many of these fathers, I wondered, were loving children who might not even be theirs? How many had been lied to, just as I had?

In one afternoon, my life had changed. Was this the shock talking? Was I overreacting? Or was this bitterness my new default setting? It frightened me, how quickly grief and betrayal could harden a person.

Over the years I had met plenty of patients with unwanted pregnancies. I never asked for the backstory. I helped them as best I could. I had also worked with families desperate for children. I had always empathised with them. I knew the struggle it could be for your partner to conceive.

But now I was one of them - one of those men in the tragic stories. Only mine was worse. I had believed, for more than twenty years, that the child I raised was mine. But she wasn't.

I continued to sit staring into space. The café buzzed around me. I felt utterly alone. I hadn't felt this empty since childhood. Kathleen had once rescued me from that dark, lonely place. But now she had plunged me straight back into it.

I was nobody again. No longer really a father. Soon I feared, no longer a husband.

Only the Lonely

As I left the café, I passed a young couple with a newborn. I stopped and shook the father's hand, wishing them joy. But deep down, I couldn't stop myself thinking, 'Is that child even yours?'

I hated that voice in me. But it was there.

When I pulled into the drive, Kathleen's car was gone. So was Emily's. I checked my phone.

There were three messages.

The first, from Kathleen. She had gone to Portsmouth with a colleague to prep a witness for an upcoming case. She would be back tomorrow evening.

The second, from Emily. She was in Birmingham for the weekend, visiting a friend from university.

The third was from James Winterbourne. Checking in on me and to call him anytime.

I felt relieved. Relieved to be alone. I needed the time to calm down and process before I saw her again. The empty house also gave me access to Kathleen's office.

I walked through the house, headed upstairs, and took a long, cool shower. Then I poured myself a stiff drink and walked into her office.

Organised chaos. Files stacked; papers spread across the desk. I rarely came in here. The walls were lined with certificates and family photos - memories of a life I was beginning to question. LEGO statues, school paintings, a clay plate with all three of our handprints.

I wondered what her parents would think of her now. They had both passed away years ago, and I missed them terribly. They had adored Emily.

I sank into her chair and sobbed. We had plans. Retirement. A home in France. Maybe our own vineyard. Now all of that felt like fiction.

I opcncd the drawers. The ones on the left were locked. I didn't have a key. The ones on the right held nothing of interest, stationery, bank statements, old payslips.

Nothing that told me who Emily's father was. I knew looking was pointless. I was hardly going to come across a file labelled 'Emily's real father.' I just wanted to sneak into Kathleen's privacy like I felt she had mine.

The house was quiet. The silence pressed down on me.

Emily was gone until Sunday night. That gave me time. Time alone with Kathleen. I would confront her. I had to.

I flicked off the light and walked out.

I hadn't eaten, and now I didn't feel like drinking either. I climbed the stairs to bed, hoping that sleep might take me.

It didn't. I tossed and turned through the night.

At some point I must have drifted to sleep as when I woke, the sun was peeking through the sides of the curtains. I finally dragged myself downstairs.

There she was.

Kathleen.

Sitting at the breakfast counter, sipping coffee and flipping through a legal file. Her life at this point unchanged.

"Well, good afternoon, sleepyhead. Do you realise it's gone ten, Albie?"

"Oh. Really? I hadn't noticed. I didn't think you were back until this evening."

"Well, that was the plan. The witness dropped out. I figured I'd come home early. Emily's not back until tomorrow, so I thought we could do something together. What do you think?"

"No, Kathleen. I don't think we should do anything."

She looked up, puzzled.

"I think you should start explaining."

"Explaining? What do you mean? Albert, what's wrong? Oh my god, Albert, why are you crying?"

"I've been to see James. He told me. Now it's time you did too. Who is Emily's father, Kathleen? I want the truth."

CHAPTER THIRTY-FOUR
Marjorie

After breakfast, which consisted of freshly baked bread, fresh fruit and the finest ground coffee, and a cheeky twinkle in both our eyes, we resolved our timetable for the day. Despite the early May chill, it was a beautiful, clear, blue-sky morning, which suited me just fine. We would be sticking to my itinerary and enjoying a trip to The London Eye. Hetty was wearing her walking shoes, as was I, so we decided rather than take a taxi, we would walk.

As we stepped out, we were greeted by the two doormen, who were, as always, delightful.

"Have a fun-packed day, ladies."

"Oh, we will." shouted Hetty, with her usual over-excited approach to a new day.

"That, Marj, is how you greet people when you've just spent the night with Colin Firth, having not had much sleep!" She winked at me, and I found myself winking back, in acknowledgment of a night well spent with Alan Titchmarsh, without a watering can in sight.

She linked her arm through mine, and we walked towards the river, laughing like we knew a secret nobody else was party to. Which of course was true.

We took our prepaid tickets to the London Eye and entered our pod together with a rather loud American family. It is hard to avoid listening to other people's conversations in a confined space.

Hetty sat listening to them like a student listening to a lecture. I called her over to my side of the pod and tried to engage her in the landmarks in view from the pods generous windows. She showed some interest in the Houses of Parliament and Big Ben. Her attention however, soon enough returned to the family who clearly were less than impressed with The London Eye as a tourist attraction.

I gave Hetty one of my looks in order that she not point out to them that this was the UK and not Disney Land. I knew she was tempted, I could read her like a book.

After the rather windswept trip, we returned to ground level and walked through Regent's Park, picking up takeaway coffee en route. Even visiting a Starbucks was a new experience to me and made me feel very trendy. On arriving in London, I'd seen many people racing through the station with what appeared to be an obligatory cup of coffee, and now I could count myself in their numbers, even if I moved at a more sociable pace.

When we entered the coffee shop, there was a whole array of coffees, some, or in fact most, of which I had simply never heard of. I could never have imagined that ordering a simple coffee could be so complex that it required a menu. I avoided the Frappuccino, macchiato or mocha (whatever they were) and simply ordered a black coffee with hot milk.

Regent's Park was delightful, with the most amazingly well-groomed flower beds and topiary, together with fountains, a lake, and even its own zoo. I thought of Alan Titchmarsh and how much he would appreciate the vast selection of trees and bushes and plants. I found myself hiding a cheeky green when his name wandered into my mind – again!

What a night we'd had.

In what seemed like no time at all, we were making our way to The Ritz for afternoon tea. We had brought smart shoes with us so we could at least change our footwear before entering and, thankfully, due to our pelvic floors holding up so well, we did not need to change anything else.

The Palm Court would be where we would be dining, and we were shown to our seats by a beautiful French girl called Claudette, who fussed over us like we were her long-lost aunts. Hetty attempted to use some French she had learnt at the French club I had tried to start at Beachcombers. I had read in The National Geographic that learning a new language was a good way to stave off dementia. Sadly, the club disbanded after about six weeks in preference for Scrabble Club, which would be conducted entirely in English.

Hetty got off to an appalling start, asking for the ladies' room in a combination of Spanish and French:

'Pour va for la toilette?'

Thankfully, Claudette, who was no doubt very used to this kind of attempt at politeness, simply showed Hetty to the bathroom while I took my seat and marvelled at the feel and atmosphere of the place, or, as they say in France, l'ambience.

The sandwiches, the pastries, the cakes were all delicious. This was just the epitome of class and sophistication. We were surrounded by London's elite and, while I took in the beautiful décor, the exquisite porcelain and the paintings, Hetty was busy celebrity-spotting, but sadly, for her at least, with no joy at all.

After two hours of being totally spoilt, we left the restaurant and walked around the areas of the hotel where non-residents were allowed to wander. Quite beautiful.

As we walked through reception Hetty commented, "Imagine being so rich that this was just normal for you."

There were lots of people busily checking in or checking out, with children nonchalantly playing around suitcases and chasing each other around the sofas and chairs that occupied the reception area. As a child, I could never have imagined being able to afford to stay in even the Sunrise Hotel, where I worked, never mind The Ritz in London, yet for these children, it was clearly normal.

We decided, having eaten so much, we would go back to our own hotel for an afternoon power nap before dining early in Covent Garden. We ambled back, busily chatting about the following morning and the meeting with my private detective, Harry. He had sent a text message to me to confirm that he would join us in the restaurant after we had finished our breakfast.

Hetty was just what I've needed on this trip. Her playful, childlike behaviour kept me amused and distracted.

Just to emphasise that point, I don't doubt for one minute that it was Colin Firth she was going back to.

Not a nap.

CHAPTER THIRTY-FIVE
Hetty

After our afternoon tea, Marjorie suggested we retire to our rooms for a well-earned nap before going out again later. She went a rather rich shade of red and giggled when I suggested she really wanted to spend a playful afternoon with Alan Titchmarsh. I did further point out to her that we would both need to register with a slimming club on our return to Cornwall given how much food and drink we were getting through.

I laid my head on the soft pillows, kicked my shoes off and in the silence, grew tearful about how lucky I was to have a friend like Marjorie.

There were just so many times when it was the depths of our friendship that had gotten one of us through a trauma for there not to be a cosmic pull defining its strength.

Since the dreadful tragedy caused by Edwin, for which he paid the ultimate price, I was alone in the house for the first time with any degree of permanency. However, despite my forced lone status, I no longer felt alone. I felt optimistic for the future.

It was as if the belt of angst and terror that had been holding me back had been loosened and I could breathe easy again. I felt such simple joy in being able to go to see Marjorie and not fear what I would be walking back into on my return home. The house would be as I'd left it. Clean, organised, and peaceful. I could now invite Marjorie to my house without apologising for Edwin's rude behaviour or without needing to usher her out before he saw her. Such a simple yet perfect luxury.

Some months after Edwin's funeral, Marjorie and I

received an invitation to come and view the plans for a small mobile home park on the land overlooking the bay in Trellinick. It was land owned by the Pensbury's, a family well-known in the village. Millys's parents had operated the ten-acre plot as a commercial small holding, producing vegetables for local pubs and restaurants but also for the villagers from their farm shop. Not a massive undertaking and not one Simon and Milly were keen to continue after Milly's parents passed away.

The hotel they inherited however, adjacent to the site and where Majorie had worked so many moons ago, was a project they were keen to develop. They had wanted to increase the number of rooms from ten to fifteen and fully renovate and modernise the entire property. That project now complete they turned their minds to the site of the small holding.

In keeping with their passion for supporting the local community, they decided to develop the small holding site as a modest and exclusive mobile home park.

I was keen to go along and listen to their plans, as was Marjorie. There were about thirty people at the meeting, the vast majority of whom were couples from the village, but as I scanned the room I noted there were a few unfamiliar faces. The meeting was held in their beautiful garden, which looked straight out to sea and, on an evening as beautiful as this, would only serve to help in their marketing campaign.

On the lawn were neat rows of fold-up chairs and at the front of the chairs was a small stage made from pallets with plywood boards on the top, covered with fake grass. A microphone and a large board with 'Beachcombers' written across it occupied the stage.

'Ooh, Beachcombers I liked the sound of that'.

As we entered their living room, there standing in the corner with a small glass of orange juice, was a rather handsome-looking gentleman, with a pocket watch and tweed suit and a tie that looked like it was made of silk.

When Marjorie noticed me clock him, she gave me a firm nudge with her elbow and said, "Will you behave yourself? He's probably the architect or planner or something like that. This is a meeting about our future residences, not a speed-dating evening."

"Well, you can't blame me for looking, Marj, he's really rather dashing, don't you think?" "Hetty, stop it, behave yourself."

We smiled playfully at each other and went across to Milly Pensbury, who handed us a rather swanky brochure with 'Beachcombers' emblazoned across the front. I smiled at our mystery man who, as we took our seats, came over and introduced himself as Albert Hargraves and asked if he could sit by us, if that wasn't too much trouble.

His perfect English accent certainly did not belong in Cornwall and was more akin to the Royal Family than our little village. He had the kindest face and was so cute and polite, we were delighted for him to sit with us. He reminded me in his demeanour and looks of Nigel Havers and, once we got talking to him further, the similarity was just cemented. He literally could have been Nigel Havers or at least Nigel Havers' brother.

The meeting was mostly hosted by an architect, who discussed in great detail the plans Milly and Simon had for the land at the back of their property. It was awesome. A brand-new mobile home park called Beachcombers, with the homes being offered to local people and friends of Milly and Simon who had expressed an interest. It would be on a first-come, first-served basis. They went to great lengths to say these were mobile homes - not caravans. That somehow made them sound more permanent, not merely a holiday home.

He showed us all an artist's impression of what the site would look like and the views across the bay that the horseshoe layout would afford all the homes. I kept touching Marjorie's knee I was so excited about it all. She didn't seem to mind at all, as at least it wasn't our new friend Albert's knee I was touching.

Planning permission had already been approved so work on the site could commence quite soon. There would be twelve homes, and they would have access to the bay via a private lane, a road would be constructed to allow access on and off the site, with a car parking space for every home. The shop at the entrance to the park would also be extended to offer more services and provisions.

By the time the evening was over, we had both booked a home. It was exactly what we both needed. A fresh start and the chance to live literally within a stone's throw of each other. The plan was for the construction to be complete towards the end of 2011, with a view to us all moving in at the beginning of 2012.

Our new friend Albert held onto his information pack and giggled at what Marjorie described to him as 'my childish enthusiasm'. Obviously, we both needed to sell ours houses first and put some money aside, but the point was I was sure we could afford to buy one of these homes and how thrilling was that?

I grabbed hold of Albert's arm and said, 'Well what do you think, Albert Hargraves, are you going to be joining us?'

"Do you know what ladies, I think I might. I have some matters I need to attend to at home and that may take the time it will take to construct this place, but I think I would really benefit from being down here with the fresh air and those views."

"Well, that settles it then, to us and our brave new beginnings. We all raised our glasses and sipped the fizz in celebration.

"Would you like to take a note of my number, Albert, you know, while you're away you can always call me for an update."

"Oh, for goodness' sake, Hetty, I am sorry, Albert, she's just so forward, isn't she? Please don't feel you have to share your personal number. Hetty, come on, leave the poor man alone. I'm sure Milly will keep him updated."

"No no, that's a jolly good idea, I'm more than happy to leave you my number. You're quite right, Milly has been keeping me up to speed with everything, but another contact down here would be greatly appreciated - especially if we're going to be neighbours."

"So how do you know Milly, Albert?"

"We were at med school together, back in the day. She is the only one from my university days I have stayed in contact with - well, besides my wife that is. Medicine, as it turns out, was not for Milly. She came back here, married Simon and ran the small holding and hotel. Of course I'm sure you know all this."

"Ooh, med school. Are you a doctor, Albert?'

"Yes, but I'm about to retire. I'm sadly separated from my wife, so I just need some time to gather myself together and sort out who I am again, you know? This place would be perfect. I've known about the plans for quite some time. I haven't just decided tonight."

"Ah, Albert, I'm on my own too so there's something else we have in common."

"Something else?"

"Yes, something else - we both live here now, don't we?'

"Hetty, that is quite enough. Albert, it was delightful to meet you and no doubt over the coming year we will see you again for visits or progress reports. Come on, Hetty, let's hand these applications into Milly and give Albert some peace. Don't you think these look like Huff Houses Hetty? Remember from Grand Designs with the fabulous Kevin McCloud."

"Huff Houses. Marjorie Hepburn you are priceless. They are mobile homes. Gorgeous mobile homes granted but hardly Huff Houses."

We laughed at the upgrading of our properties as we handed our completed applications in. By the end of the evening, all the homes were reserved, it was definitely happening.

The softness of the pillows and the stillness of room both combined to result in me drifting off.

I woke with the tv remote in one hand and pins and needles in the other. It hadn't been my intention to drop off, but a day on the move, wine and fatigue had clearly got the better of me. I sent Marjorie a text and she had doubtless also fallen the same way as I did not receive a reply.

Unless she was busy with Mr Titchmarsh of course, in which case I was very glad I hadn't disturbed her.

CHAPTER THIRTY-SIX
Albert

The room was still. The air felt thick in my throat. Kathleen walked to the French windows and opened them. She stood in the doorway, arms wrapped around her waist, gazing out at the garden we had built together. Once for a child, now filled with hardy shrubs and layered memories. The air in the room was still and I remember feeling a thick, cloying sensation in my throat.

She had planted the trees with me when we first bought the house and had laid the borders with a young child in mind to start with, but as time passed, with hardier heathers, cacti and rose bushes. She'd loved her garden and equally loved how it had been an evolving project over time; one we had all enjoyed together.

"I'm so sorry, Albert. I cannot begin to tell you how sorry I am. I'm sorry it happened. I'm sorry you have discovered the truth and I'm even more sorry for the reason you have uncovered the truth. That it took Emily to become so desperately unwell for you to find out."

She sat down once again and, having taken several sips of her coffee, she began. '

"What do you want to know, Albert?"

"Who is the father?" Before you say another word, I want to know his name."

"It was Harvey's brother, Charlie. Harvey doesn't even know Albert, so you cannot blame him. I cannot tell you how sorry I am, you have to believe me, but it was once. Just once and it meant nothing to me. I was stupid, and selfish and drunk and if I could turn the clock back I would, but I can't. I've lived with this all these years.'

"Charlie McBride? Are you for real? Emily's father is Charlie McBride!"

"Albert I'm so sorry. I hate myself for this."

"Oh please, I hope you don't expect me to feel sorry for you, carrying this all these years. Charlie, for Christ's sake Kathleen, Charlie! That means Harvey is more related to Emily than I am. She's his niece. I bet he's known all this time. No wonder they moved so soon after Emily was born. He couldn't stand the guilt at looking at his niece."

I could feel anger building in me. These feelings were entirely new to me, and I was struggling to know how to contain my emotions.

"Is that why you didn't go to Charlie's funeral. Too ashamed of the part you played in his life. Too ashamed to face his wife and daughters and show sympathy? Oh, sorry for your loss Agnes but his other daughter is doing fine. The daughter you know nothing about.

I can't believe I'm hearing this. He was our neighbour's brother. That slimy bastard. Did he lie in my bed, in our bed and impregnate my wife because I wasn't man enough to?"

"No, Albert, no. Don't say that. You are every bit the man I married and loved. It didn't happen here. It was when I was in Scotland. I had been away at one of the conferences I went to at that time in Edinburgh. I don't expect you to remember this specific one, there were so many back then.

I'd had a pig of a week, and honestly wanted to come home at several points, but I'd committed to stay. Charlie lived in Edinburgh at the time. We met in the bar of my hotel. We had dinner and drinks.

I don't know how or why it happened, but I invited him to my room. It was not my intention to sleep with him, Albert, I promise you. I was just enjoying his company after such an intense week. But I did sleep with him. I did and I am beyond sorry. When I then realised I was pregnant, I couldn't possibly know if the baby was yours or his. I have carried this for all these years and prayed, I or we, would never need to know who the father was.

To me it was you."

Kathleen stayed sat down with her hands tightly knitted together and her body arched forward. I remember I got up from my seat and walked over to the sink and turned on the tap. The cool water rushed into the sink like a vortex, spinning around the corners before circling into the middle and disappearing.

I poured myself a glass of cool water without looking at her and without saying a word. I stayed with my head lowered and my weight propped heavily against the unit.

"Did he spend the whole night with you?"

"No. He left in the small hours. Oh, Albert, I'm so incredibly sick, telling you this. Please will you ever forgive me?"

"Why Kathleen? Why? We were so happy then, or so I thought. We were trying for a baby for Christ's sake. Of course, you could get pregnant by him. You haven't just taken any trust we had, or sense of loyalty. You have stolen my identity. I thought I was a father, but it turns out I am not.

"No, Albert, you cannot say that. I knew you wanted to be a father just as desperately as I wanted to be a mother, but it just wasn't happening for us. Month after month we failed to become pregnant, and it was slowly killing me. I didn't know or understand why, whether I was the problem or you. When we went to the fertility clinic, I think we both knew what the doctor was saying when he said your sperm count was low. I felt sure he was just letting us down gently. It wasn't happening, Albert, how long were we going to have to keep trying?

It was an incredibly stupid and selfish thing to do I understand that now. I became pregnant, Albert, and I gave you what you wanted. What we both wanted, a child. It wasn't planned or anything like that, but I guess in my desperation, I just let it happen and didn't think about the long-term consequences.

I didn't take fatherhood away from you Albie, I gave it to you. If Emily had not become so ill, you would never have known. I would never have known whether she was yours or his. I got to a point where I stopped even thinking about whether she was yours or his. To me she is yours and will always be yours. She's our girl, Albert.

But then Emily got sick and when you first expressed real concerns for Em's health, I sent samples to a lab for DNA testing. It was obvious from your anxiety that this was not just a trivial illness. When the results came back, I was devastated. I had always held on to the wish that you were the biological father. It was clear that was not the case.

I promise you, Albert, this happened only once, and I cannot find the words to say how sorry I am that I have hurt you with this secret. I have only known a few weeks longer than you, Albert, and this has always been my fear.

But do you know what, Albie? If the alternative to this is that Emily didn't happen and we missed out on being parents, then I'm glad of what happened that night. Em is as much a blessing today, with the knowledge of who her real father is, as she was before it was uncovered."

"What a strange moral compass you have, Kathleen. What a way to justify an affair by offering it up to me as a gift. As something I should be grateful for. I was incapable of getting my wife pregnant, so along comes Charlie-boy and he does the job for me and presents me with a daughter. Am I supposed to be grateful, Kathleen? Is that really what you're saying?

When a doctor tells you your sperm count is low, that's what it means. Low. He didn't say 'impossible.' You don't just assume from that 'poor Albert can't do it so I'll sleep with someone else who can make babies, then I will just lie about it forever'. There were lots of options open to us, Kathleen. Lots of treatments we hadn't even explored. We could have adopted together, for God's sake. You don't just decide 'I'll give Albert what he wants and sleep with a different man'. What are you even suggesting that for?

No, I can see exactly what you're doing here, Kathleen, and I'm not buying it at all. You are twisting this to be my fault and that's not fair or true. Then you expect me to be pleased or grateful of your clever plan to give me a child."

"No, Albert, I'm not saying that at all, I'm saying that

we clearly couldn't make a baby together. Albert, we tried. For years we tried and got nowhere. When I became pregnant, I didn't know for sure whether the baby was yours or his. I'm just saying that now we know it is his. Without that one night, Emily would not be here, so I'm glad of that at least. Oh god, I'm not asking you to be grateful, Albie. Em is your girl and will always be your girl

"Did Charlie know he could be the father?"

"I told him, yes. He was desperately shocked and upset, obviously. I felt I had to tell him. Not because I wanted anything from him, I just thought he should know. When you came home from work and told me that Charlie had died in terrible car crash, I simply couldn't believe it.

You're right, there was no way I could attend his funeral and watch his wife and daughters grieve for him. He was not the man they thought he was. I'm sure I wasn't the first woman he'd slept with whilst married to Agnes. Saying that, I'm sure I am no longer the wife you thought I was. Can you ever forgive me Albert?"

"I cannot believe this Kathleen, I honestly cannot believe any of it. You have ripped my fucking heart out and stamped on it. How dare you ask for my forgiveness. Forgive you for what exactly, Kathleen? Which part of this fucking pack of lies and deceit do you want me to forgive you for? That I found out? That you went away for work and slept with someone because you were drunk? That he got you pregnant and for over twenty years you kept it from me. Do you expect me to believe a word you say?

Maybe this happened more than once. How do I know you didn't get drunk at every conference you went away to and took a fellow drinker back to your room? How do I know Kathleen, tell me, how do I fucking know? How can I trust a darn word that comes out of your lying mouth?"

Kathleen was now slumped in the chair, crying. She raised her head to meet my eyes, but as she did so I turned my back to her and walked over to the breakfast bar and sat down kneading my hands together. After a short pause I looked across to Kathleen.

I couldn't bare her tears. I couldn't bear that I had spoken with such hatred to her. She was the only woman I had loved. She had laid herself bare to me and finally admitted the lie she had kept for over twenty years. Life until this point had never asked me to search for forgiveness. I had never been so horribly wronged before. And yet, maybe Kathleen was right. We had Emily. Where in all of my hateful words was she? Kathleen was still Emily's mother after all, even if I was not her father.

"Does Emily know? Am I the only one who knows nothing of this? Don't even say Harvey doesn't know. He knows. Charlie and he were incredibly close. Charlie would have told him that he'd slept with you at least. That means Morag knows. No wonder you two drifted apart. Not distance. Secrets. I hate that Harvey has this over me. Has always had this over me. I feel sick. This is just too much Kathleen, I honestly cannot believe you could do this to me, to us. Now I find out that you created this mess with our neighbour's brother and your best friend's brother-in-law."

"Emily is not a mess, Albert, please don't say that. I told you; I did this for you. Yes, for me too, but I was thinking about you."

"What! What the hell are you saying Kathleen, spending the night with him but thinking about me? Are you saying that to sugar coat this, to make it less sordid, less of a crime to our marriage? There is nothing 'less' about this, Kathleen. You didn't just cheat, you lied and deceived me, and were you thinking about me all those years you were doing that? I very much doubt it.

What is clear from all of this, Kathleen, is that you only cared about yourself. You got what you wanted. To hell with how you got it. You wanted it so badly you just slept with Charlie and lied to us all until fate caught you out. If Emily had not become so ill, you would have continued with this deception. Your tears for Emily were not solely for her, were they? They were for you too, and the fact that the game was up."

"I did a terrible thing, Albert, I admit that. A truly terrible thing and for the hurt this is causing you I am truly sorry. But you have to believe me, if I hadn't done

this, there would be no Emily, there would ne
been an Emily. It wasn't happening for us, Albu
know that just as much as I do.

It was the worst kind of deception, I know that
actually the sex with Charlie, the act itself, me ...t
nothing. I felt nothing for him. You must believe me. He
wanted to continue after I returned from Scotland, but I
made it clear I did not. It wasn't an affair. It was a stupid,
selfish, drink-fuelled night. A means to an end and
nothing more.

When I returned from Edinburgh I obviously didn't even
know that I was pregnant."

I couldn't quite take in what Kathleen was telling me. I
sat at the breakfast bar with my hands covering my eyes.
I am not a violent or aggressive man but in those
moments, I just wanted to punch something.

I felt absolutely in the dark as to what I truly meant to
her. I was the disappointing husband who couldn't get
her pregnant. Charlie the unfortunate lover who could. I
thought at several points that I would be sick as I
pictured Charlie entwined with my wife. That his hands
had known her, and his mouth had tasted her.

It was making my insides writhe in pain. Yet looking at
her, crying and curled into herself, I had to fight the urge
to go to her and comfort her. My mind went to Emily.
She was a victim in all of this too.

"Have you told Emily. Is that really why she isn't here?"

"No, I haven't told her. I knew this was something we
should tell her together. I know there are enough secrets
now, Albert, but I am so frightened that telling her now
when she is doing so well with her treatment might just
upset the whole process and she will end up ill again.
Please, Albert, we can't risk that. We need to try our best
to keep Emily in recovery. I know completely she
deserves to know the truth, but don't you think we
should wait? What is there to be gained by telling her
this now?"

There was no question that telling Emily would be a
devastating shock for her and one she could do without
just now. But I also hated her being lied to and duped
any longer than she and I had already been by her

mother. I needed to take stock of everything Kathleen had just told me and decide whether I could be around her. Emily was so close to us both. I didn't doubt she would immediately pick up on an atmosphere between us. My beautiful Emily.

How much more pain could life throw at her?

I looked across at Kathleen.

Picked up my glass.

Left the kitchen to breathe thinner air.

CHAPTER THIRTY-SEVEN
Marjorie

Our evening entertainment began early with dinner in Covent Garden. This was to be a new experience for me as I had never eaten in an Italian restaurant before. Hetty was maintaining she had, but I made it clear I was not accepting Pizza Hut as authentic Italian cuisine simply on the basis it sold pizza.

The meal was yet again delicious. The staff had fussed over us and actually some of the other diners sitting close to us advised us both what we should order, based on their previous experiences. I ordered the ravioli, which was the best I had ever tasted, and Hetty had venison ragu. We managed to polish off the best part of two bottles of the finest pinot grigio, and a cocktail each to start so we were both quite tipsy.

It was whilst we were eating our dessert that I first noticed the two women staring at us. Well maybe they weren't staring, but they were certainly looking more than was socially acceptable in our direction. I subtly pointed them out to Hetty who, typically less than subtly, stared back at them both and reported through a slurred and somewhat raised voice that she didn't think they were anything to worry about.

I kept my eye on the two women however, as whilst they outwardly appeared to be chatting companionably with each other, I could see a mobile phone on their table and feared we were being filmed or recorded. I decided that we wouldn't stay for more drinks and asked for the bill and our coats together with a taxi.

The waiter returned with the bill, as usual in a neat little folder and a card machine. I obviously declined the machine, placing the requisite amount of cash plus a tip in the folder and handed it back to him. He simply thanked us for our custom, handed us our coats and informed us that our taxi was outside.

I got up from the table to use the facilities before our departure, and on my return was horrified to see Hetty chatting with the afore mentioned women. They were all giggling, no doubt at something inappropriate Hetty had said, and when she saw me gesture for her to join me, she gave them both a hug and we made our way to the door and our awaiting taxi.

As we climbed into the taxi, I asked the driver to take us to The Savoy, and I turned to Hetty. Before I could say anything else Hetty quickly remarked, "You know what they say Marjorie, keep your friends close, and your enemies closer. Nothing to fear from those two women Marj, nothing at all. They are sisters down in London celebrating a birthday. Tourists the same as us."

I didn't bother to point out to her that even if they were secretly following us, they were hardly likely to announce it in the middle of a restaurant. In any event, I probably was just being paranoid though I did check no other taxis left the restaurant heading in the same direction as us.

Hetty noticed me checking and as I turned back to face her the pair of us just burst out laughing. Subtlety not being her strong suit, she said rather too loudly she was going to pee her pants - again. As we left the cab, I didn't check if she had, and frankly I didn't want to know. How had I gone from lemon tea and breakfast on an isolated beach in Cornwall, to an imaginary film set where we were being followed by gangsters across London?

We arrived back at the hotel, gathered our composure, and made our way to the famous American Bar for a night cap. Hetty had not had the accident she feared she might have had in the taxi, so changes of clothes were not necessary. In truth, we had probably had enough alcohol and excitement for one night, but Hetty was keen to try a few of the cocktails she had read about in the room information folder. I was keen to go there just to say I had seen it and sampled a cocktail too. I also wanted to stay on track with the itinerary. The following morning was to be our Breakfast at Tiffany's experience and of course our date with Harry and the new information he had uncovered about my William.

I thought it would be a good idea to go to bed very tired and, if need be, very tipsy, so that the weight of excitement and anticipation for what Harry was about to tell me about William didn't keep me awake. A vein hope I was sure.

There was an electric buzz in the place when we arrived. A pianist was playing and though not all tables were full, there was a generous crowd of very happy guests drinking and chatting. We sat down at a table near the bar and, having studied the menu, ordered two cocktails. I decided upon a 'Somewhere Sailin'' as it reminded me of home and Hetty went for an 'Electric Lover,' which she playfully dedicated to the purchases we had made at Ann Summers the day before.

They were amazing cocktails and before long we were singing along with the pianist and the other 'cocktail quaffers' as he played songs from movies of the fifties and sixties.

With our drinks almost finished, the waiter came over to our table with two more. I was about to say that I was sorry, we hadn't ordered more, when he announced, "Ladies, the gentleman at the bar has sent these drinks over to you and wondered if he could join you?" Again, I was about to say no as we were going to retire but before I could, Hetty had leant back, raised her glass to him and told the waiter, "Of course, that would be delightful."

As the waiter turned to him and signalled our agreement, (when I say 'our', I mean 'Hetty's'), he picked up his drink and came over and joined us.

"Good evening, ladies. I've noticed you both around the hotel these past few days. Let me introduce myself to you, I am Brodie Harpington-Smythe. What might your names be?"

Hetty giggled like a child replying, "Do you want to know what our names really are or what they might be?"

I sat there and listened as she beamed at his flattery and

told him our real names and not what they might be - what a strange thing to say, anyway. As they chatted about why he was at the hotel (no doubt lies) and why he was chatting to two women he didn't know about his life (also no doubt lies). I stopped Hetty from telling him too much about where we lived and quickly interjected,

"We both live in Huff Houses in an exclusive development in north Cornwall, don't we Hetty? I know about Huff Houses from a Channel Four programme called Grand Designs, which I occasionally watch at Hetty's Huff House. I personally don't watch Channel Four, I prefer the BBC, but Hetty does like it, don't you?"

Brodie looked from me and to Hetty somewhat confused but then smiled and replied,

"Well Huff Houses are quite the thing, aren't they? How marvellous that you should both live in one."

After nearly an hour of engaging in light-hearted conversation with Brodie, I grew to enjoy his company, and it goes almost without saying that Hetty was in her element. He was incredibly sweet and whilst at first, I was concerned he was merely interested in an illicit night with one of us whilst away from his wife on business, it turned out I could not have been more wrong.

He was a widower and was in London to visit his son who was at university studying engineering. After two further cocktails, we both thanked him for his company explaining we had a full and busy day ahead and made our way back to our rooms. Not before Hetty had a selfie with him and made a note of his number, as I know he did hers.

As I prepared for bed I received a text from Hetty. Very simple but so touching.

Tomorrow is for you Marjorie. I hope with all my heart you hear good news. H x

I held the phone close to my chest and wished the same for myself. It had been so many years. Could this be the start of something incredible or would it be the end of the line for my dreams of being with William again?

I woke at six, as I had on previous mornings, ready to take my little walk down the Thames simply to clear my mind, but before I left I sent a little text to Hetty just to check she was awake. She responded at once that she was and that she would see me at reception at eight. I packed my suitcase and left out the clothes I would be wearing after I had showered on my return. I set off toward the Thames with a whole array of thoughts and emotions racing through my mind.

I was so excited to be finally experiencing Breakfast at Tiffany's and at the prospect of losing myself in the timeless imagery of my namesake and lifelong obsession with Audrey Hepburn. Of course, I was also a mess of emotion about what I was going to be hearing about my boy William. Whenever it came back into my mind, a little surge of either excitement or trepidation took over my breathing and I felt almost sick.

When I got back to the room I quickly showered and dressed and packed my last few bits and pieces into my new wheelie suitcase. The last, let's call it, 'item', to be packed away was the purchase from Ann Summers. The evening, I had spent with it (AKA Alan Titchmarsh), certainly was liberating, and had taken me to places I had only imagined. But did I really want to take it back to Cornwall?

The problem was, what else could I do with it now? I didn't want to put it in the bin in the room, and I certainly wasn't going to carry it around the hotel with me until I found a bin - what if it went off over my eggs benedict? The only solution was that I should bring it home with me. At least then I could decide whether to keep it or discard it in my bins. Lord only knows which bin I should put it in, and was it even recyclable?

At eight o'clock I made my way downstairs to reception where Hetty was already seated waiting for me. She told me her heart had skipped a beat this morning as when she woke, Brodie had sent her a message. He'd left the hotel and was travelling home to Chester but hoped she would stay in touch with him. I shook my head at her as she grabbed hold of me, and we laughed about it like silly schoolgirls as we waited at reception to be checked out.

Our two doormen hailed a taxi for us and, with so much excitement and anticipation I thought I might burst, we set off to have breakfast with my hero. I had purposefully worn a fitted dress with a matching jacket with my hair brushed back and bright red lipstick. I'd earlier looked at myself in the mirror and whispered, 'This is for you, Audrey Hepburn, and all the joy, the escapism and pleasure you have given me. But it is also for you William. Let this be an exciting beginning."

Hetty looked stunning too in navy three-quarter-length trousers, cream polo neck jumper, trench coat and red kitten-heel shoes. She borrowed my red lipstick to complete the look. I must say, we looked divine. As we entered Harrods, we followed the directions to the café and as I was greeted by an image of Audrey Hepburn on the wall, a sudden flood of tears came over me.

"Why was I born when I was, Hetty? Too late to have been your friend Audrey? Why did I never meet you? How were you so totally beautiful and brilliant? Look at her, Hetty, just look at her."

We were welcomed by a waitress at the entrance, and I confirmed that I had made a booking for two people in the name of Marjorie Hepburn - "Sadly, no relation."

She smiled back at me and said, "Really? You could have been sisters, Audrey, and Marjorie Hepburn."

I loved the very thought of that. She showed us to our table and immediately offered us some tea. I was just in a whirl. I drifted back to the sixties, surrounded by Tiffany blue walls and décor with images of Audrey Hepburn looking absolutely stunning swimming around in my mind. As we sat down, Hetty took a framed photograph of Audrey Hepburn from her handbag and sat it on the table. "Well, Marjorie, if we're having Breakfast at Tiffany's, we need Audrey to join us, don't we?"

How perfect was that?

We ate a delicious breakfast of eggs Florentine with

smoked salmon, together with bowls of fresh fruit and the most incredible freshly baked bread. Hetty was typically supportive and didn't come up for air talking. She understood that I was totally distracted by what I was about to find out from Harry. I forgave her for her non-stop chatter, which as I recall, included the name Brodie on several occasions.

After we had been in the restaurant about an hour, I looked up from Hetty, and there standing at the entrance was a very handsome gentleman in a suit, talking to a waitress. They both looked across at us, so I knew this was it. This was Harry, and I was about to discover what had happened to my son.

William.

My boy.

The reason I have kept going.

CHAPTER THIRTY-EIGHT
Harry

I arrived in London at 3pm the day before I was due to meet my most enigmatic of clients to date. After I had left CID twelve years earlier, I had set my agency up and had never looked back. A mixture of the joy my work generally gave my clients and the freedom I had to pick and choose my clients, was what spurred me forward.

I hadn't actually met Marjorie May Hepburn, but I felt a strange attachment to her, or at least to her story. We hadn't spoken; communication had been limited to email. I had tried to introduce Marjorie to video calling, but she had been reluctant on the basis that 'anonymity was a much-underrated concept in the modern world'. I had no understanding of what she meant then, as I don't now, but Majorie is a woman who clearly knows her own mind, so video calling was off.

I checked into my hotel in central London and once safely unpacked and orientated into my new surroundings, I showered and changed into more casual jogging pants and a sweatshirt. My room was comfortable with the warmth of the May sun casting deep shadows across the floor, creeping slowly up the walls.

Marjorie's file was both complex and heart-breaking. Sadly, a story all too familiar in cases I had dealt with from that era. A reflection of how things were back then. So many children were taken from their mothers simply because they were born out of wedlock, or the mothers were considered too young and therefore incapable of keeping the child. It was often the Church that intervened in these cases, representing a cruel irony to their teachings of love and respect to all from all. Marjorie's story, however, and the character I now knew her to be had, captured something in me.

She was unaware but I had engaged in several conversations with her close friend Albert. He had helped enormously with details relating to William's removal; possibly details too painful for Marjorie to recount. I had been so moved by what Albert told me about Marjorie and their cosy living arrangements in Cornwall. I had been able to Facetime Albert, a man not quite so disturbed by modern technology clearly. I had seen his beautiful home and through his windows, how close he lived to Marjorie and their other friend Hetty. Once my investigations were concluded, I hoped I could visit them in person. I just had to hope that the outcome was a positive one.

I had never worked with a client before where I hadn't insisted on at least a part payment up front, but I had made an exception with Marjorie who had told me straight. "Now Mr Stavely, Harry, I will not be sending you fees online. I do not work that way. You have said your services will be fifteen thousand pounds. Well, I will pay you of course but you will only be paid at the end of your investigations in cash, no questions asked, and only when you reveal all the avenues you have explored. Ideally when I am sitting opposite my son sipping tea."

Unbelievable! I had laughed at the time. I was being dictated to by this awesome lady, but honestly, she had crept inside my head. By the time she had fully explained her story, and the injustice of it all, I was as keen to help her discover where her son was as she was. I happily assumed that her desire to settle her bill with cash rather than electronically was merely a reflection of her hesitance to use technology, be that social media platforms or on-line banking.

I had arranged to meet Marjorie with her friend Hetty at the Blue Box Café in Harrods at eleven o'clock, by which time the ladies would have finished their breakfast experience. It seems this was to be a special occasion for Marjorie, who had some sort of life-long obsession with Audrey Hepburn. They were enjoying a

Breakfast at Tiffany's as an homage to her love for the actress.

I knew enough about them from my many telephone conversations with Albert, to know that the beautifully well-groomed, elegant looking women in the corner booth with an air of Audrey Hepburn about them was indeed Marjorie and Hetty. The waitress at the entrance to the café took me across to meet the ladies, who she knew were waiting for a gentleman to join them. She then noted my order for an Americano while refreshing the ladies' order of two English breakfast teas.

I shook hands with both ladies and confidently introduced myself as Harry Stavely from The Child Reunions Agency and confirmed that I was delighted to finally meet them both. Marjorie looked at Hetty, who took hold of her dear friend's hand. It was Hetty who spoke first.

"This is going to be very emotional, Mr Stavely, as you can imagine. Marjorie has been waiting a lifetime to find this out, I'm sure you will understand that."

"Of course I do, totally. Please call me Harry and, Marjorie, I want you to know I will stop at any point, and I will stay here with you ladies as long as you need me to. Today I am totally yours. There is no rush. I find this can be emotional for any number of reasons, so I totally understand."

Marjorie lent down to her handbag and pulled out a packet of tissues, and a large brown envelope, clearly filled with the money she was about to hand over for my services. She even took the trouble to pull the envelope open so I could see the stash of notes inside. She handed me the envelope stating that she wanted the formalities dealt with from the outset. That way she could then regard the upcoming conversation as being amongst friends, rather than a formal interaction between a client and a service provider.

As I placed the envelope into my briefcase, she continued, "Now, I will not be offended if you choose to count it out, but I can assure you there is fifteen thousand pounds in that envelope Harry."

I smiled back at Marjorie. Hetty remained silent and kept

hold of Marjorie's hand. It was clear to me that the news they were both about to hear had deeply affected her too. The waitress returned to our table as I opened the file and went through paperwork requiring Marjorie's signature, which was witnessed by Hetty and then countersigned. As the waitress walked away, I began.

"Marjorie, on the 15th of April 1972, in Trellinick, North Cornwall, you gave birth to a baby boy - William Anchorage. He was taken from you by your mother on the 25th of April 1972 when he was just ten days old and placed with a family who subsequently adopted him. If those dates are correct, I can now tell you that I have been able to locate him."

I remember the look of pain and distress on Marjorie's face as she confirmed those dates and events to be correct.

I hoped I was about to give her the news she had waited a lifetime to hear.

CHAPTER THIRTY-NINE
Albert

It was when I was alone with Emily, watching her move around my home, fussing, cooking, moving my ornaments to what she would assure me were better suited places, that I saw how much like her mother she was. She caught me smiling at her repositioning my baking and bread making books. She came over and curled up next to me.

"I'm turning into mum, aren't I?"

"It's like you can read my mind Em, another one of your mum's skills."

"When did you last speak with mum? I don't mean, a quick text or call. I mean a meal together or a drink out somewhere. I don't like how distant you've become. Not just geographically. It's lovely here dad, but you're just so remote. Mum misses you so much. Can you find a way to forgive her? It's been so long, and surely if I can forgive her, you can too?"

If only I could move past the pain Kathleen caused Emily as easily as Emily could. My personal sense of betrayal was one thing, but I am still haunted by the day we told Emily who her real father was.

When Emily returned home that evening, there was an eerie silence emanating from the living room. Usually, the TV would be on with the door propped open by a sausage-dog doorstopper she had bought us when she was fourteen - another hint to us that she wanted a dog. If it wasn't the TV, it would be the sounds of Kathleen's eighties music playing in her study.

That day however, there was just silence. She shouted,

'I'm back!' as she dropped her bags at the foot of the stairs and kicked off her shoes walking through to join me. I was sitting at the breakfast bar with a small glass of whiskey slowly losing its orange hue to the melting ice cubes.

"You okay, dad? You look sad, where's mum?" She came over to me and gave me the biggest hug and realised I had clearly been crying.

"Dad, what's wrong? Where's mum, has something happened to mum?" She held onto me as she heard her mother walking into the kitchen with an equally distressed look on her face.

"Oh God, am I ill again? Have I had bad results from my blood tests? Why are you both looking like this?"

"Emily, honey, please come and sit down. There's something I, sorry we, would like to talk to you about but please don't worry, it is not to do with your bloods. In fact, I have your blood results here and they are spot on. You're actually doing marvellously."

"Why are you both looking so sad then, has somebody died?"

"No Emily, nobody has died. Your mum and I just have something very important we need to tell you. Kathleen, come and sit by Emily, it may be best if you are close to each other."

"What the hell, you two? What the hell is going on?"

I clasped my hands and again I could see tears forming in Emily's eyes. She looked frantically for a clue as to what was happening from her mum then back to me. Kathleen had her head down, her hand clutching her cheek, tears pooling in the corners of her eyes.

I then squeezed my hands and began.

"Emily, as you know we all had our bloods taken for DNA analysis for a possible transplant, should you need one. Thankfully that is looking less likely now as you are responding so well with your treatment Obviously with your initial diagnosis we needed everything in place should we need to go down that route. However, the results have revealed a rather sad truth that I, at least, was not expecting.

It seems that I am in fact not your biological father. This changes nothing, my darling. To me you are still my beautiful princess, and you always will be. Emily, look at me, this makes no difference to me at all in terms of my love for you. You have a right to know and that is why we are telling you. Kathleen, I am going to let you explain who Emily's father is."

"You are not my real dad? You've always been my real dad. There must be a mistake. I couldn't love you the way I do, if you were not real. Mum, tell him he's wrong. Tell him the DNA results are wrong. Dad, you are mine. Please, please, you are mine."

I remember then how Kathleen reached out to touch me, to comfort me, but I almost coldly brushed her hand away. Emily started to cry and simply couldn't stop. I tried to comfort her, but she had gone rigid as her tears turned to sobs.

"Is it true, mum? Who is it? Who is my real dad?"

"Emily, I am so sorry. I want you to know that I love you so much"

"Mum, stop. Just stop. Who is it? I want to know."

"It's Charlie McBride Emily, but you need to listen and try to understand, honey. Please Emily, let me explain everything to you."

The horror on her face must have told Kathleen everything. At this point at least the conversation was over. She stood up and looked at us both incredulous.

"Charlie McBride? Your friends brother?! Are you kidding me. What the hell. How? How is he my dad? I don't understand. You never dated Charlie McBride. Am I nothing more than a horrible mistake you are no doubt about to tell me you regretted. Christ, I can't be here. Was I a drunken shag, mum, or an affair? Is that what I really am? A drunken shag with your friend's brother. This is a nightmare. A total nightmare. Dad, what is she saying? How can this be true?"

As she motioned to leave the kitchen, Kathleen tried to take her hand, but she rushed past her and ran upstairs.

"Give her time Kathleen. I've had twenty-four hours to adjust to this news. She needs to take it in too. I can't even begin to imagine how this must feel for her. Maybe it would have been kinder if it were some random guy. The fact she knows her real father so well somehow probably makes it harder. The fact he is no longer with us - another added complication."

"You are her real father, Albie, don't ever say you are not."

"No, Kathleen. No. I raised her, and I loved her from her first breath and always will. This changes nothing for me about my Emily. But we both know I no longer own the title of father. I will however covet 'daddy' forever

Kathleen moved closer towards me as she spoke. She looked lost. Completely lost.

"What the hell have I done? It feels like the dominoes are falling and I cannot stop the avalanche. I pushed the first slate and now all the pieces are falling and it's my fault entirely."

Emily stayed upstairs all evening. We checked on her of course. A tightly curled up bundle on the centre of her bed. I left cups of tea on her dresser and gently stroked her hair like she used to love me do as I read to her when she was little. I reassured her in as gentle a voice as I could muster that nothing had changed for me. That she was still my girl. That her mother had made a dreadful mistake but would never wish any pain on Emily or indeed on me.

In the morning, she slowly descended the stairs. She looked so tired, so lost.

she asked us both to join her in the kitchen. In silence we did. "Mum, I am ready to listen now. Dad, will you come and sit with me too. I want you here to be with me. I am sorry I said what I said last night. I was obviously just in shock. Dad, I love you the same. You are my dad, nothing will ever taint that. Charlie was nothing to me. Nothing has changed. Just biology. My body is in crisis anyway. My flesh is just a collection of cells. If they are Charlie's cells, not yours it doesn't matter. It's what's in my heart and head that matters dad, not cells.

I can't see them or feel them. I can feel what's in my heart though, and that's you. It will always be you. Charlie is dead now anyway so he will never be a father to me."

Only the Lonely

She turned to her mum and asked her to tell her everything, and Kathleen did. In detail she told her of our desperate wish for a baby and the opportunity fate had dealt them that night at the hotel in Scotland. She listened and wept as Kathleen told her of the joy we both felt at the realisation she was pregnant. Emily believed her mother when she told her it wasn't an affair and, though she didn't love Charlie, Emily was made out of love. A desperate love and desire for me to become a father and for the hope that she would be the result of the liaison.

Emily snuggled into my shoulder as if she were a child again. She kissed the top of my head and told me over and over that she loved me just the same and that nothing would change that. She looked at us both and spoke.

"I understand and though I am still in shock, I just need time. I don't agree with you lying to me and dad, that is a terrible thing to have done. But I think I understand how badly you both wanted a baby. Anyway, whatever the truth, you are my dad, always have been, always will be."

I saw it though. Overnight, things had changed. There was already an invisible wall between her mother and me. An almost imperceptible separation. My belief in the world had been shattered. My belief in Kathleen had been stolen by life and desire. Not carnal desire. A desire that she be granted what she wanted - to be a mother. She, of course, would say it was also to give me what I wanted, but the spell had been broken and the wand snapped in two.

So, Charlie's web of destruction branched out further and further. This had never been a game of winners and losers and yet I looked to have lost in a game I took no part in. Kathleen would have to accept that the fire she had played with was now burning her deeply. The chance she had taken all those years ago had finally caught up with her.

So it was that the empty cup on the empty nightstand was to prove itself a metaphor for the end of our marriage.

CHAPTER FORTY
Harry

I gathered my notes together as both Marjorie and Hetty took large gulps of their tea and gathered themselves for what I was about to tell them.

"William was taken to Exeter to live with his father, Michael Steven Anchorage, and his grandmother Clodagh Jane Anchorage."

Marjorie slumped back in her chair as Hetty gasped and grabbed hold of the arm of her dear friend.

"What?! Michael had him. That's impossible, he didn't even know I was pregnant. My boy. My beautiful boy. He was raised by his father. Are you telling me he was raised by his father? Why didn't he tell me?"

"Well not exactly, Marjorie, let me explain or would you like me to read to you a letter from William's grandmother Clodagh. She has written to you?"

"What? What do you mean 'not exactly'? Was he or wasn't he?"

"It was Clodagh Anchorage who raised him. She approached your mother to take on William's care. Let me backtrack just a little here, Marjorie. Back in the seventies, when a child was formally adopted, the papers were filed with the courts and then archived. There are ways however, of gaining access to the records. It's not easy and it took a bit of digging but I was slowly able to piece together the story.

Your mother registered William's birth, which was the correct thing to do. She used the name you had given him, which again was helpful. When he went to live with Michael's mother Clodagh in Exeter, she formally

163

adopted him when he was just three months old but with what I am going to assume were papers with your forged signature on them. I have copies of those papers here for you to keep.

Your mother had lied to Clodagh and claimed you didn't want the baby and stated you were happy to sign the adoption papers. It would appear that the adoption agency were working somewhat in collusion with your mother and just overlooked a lot of what I would say was clear evidence you were not party to this arrangement. Again, this was not uncommon at the time.

"You mentioned in your email that your mother was a churchgoer. In small communities like Trellinick, the church had incredible power and influence over its congregation. It is very likely your mother was being encouraged to expedite this adoption quickly and efficiently so that everyone could just return to their lives - as if William had never happened. As I explained, William Anchorage would then become William Michael Anchorage from July 6th, 1972. I was able to track him by his date of birth and then discovered the new parents' details.

"William lived with Clodagh until he was twenty-one. Through neighbours, I was able to establish that when she was eighty-four, Clodagh moved to Pineview Care Home in Exeter, which was where I made contact with her. I have to say, Marjorie, she is a remarkable lady and like your good self, clearly loved William with all her heart."

Marjorie was struggling to process what I was telling her. It was Hetty who broke the silence.

"But how did Clodagh even know Marjorie was pregnant and how was she so sure it was Michael's?"

"She had heard mutterings of your virtual incarceration at home and the rumour it was because you were pregnant. Despite the fact that Michael had left Trellinick to start a new life, she knew the dates would still be right for him to be the baby's father.

At the time, both Clodagh and your mother Violet attended the same weekly Women's Guild meetings and after a meeting one evening, Clodagh confronted your mother and asked if you were carrying Michael's baby.

Your mother was evidently furious and told her to mind her business. Clodagh wouldn't let it go and said that everyone knew you were pregnant and that if the baby was Michael's, she had a right to know. Violet then told her you were pregnant. It was Michael's baby, but that you had realised it was a terrible mistake and that you were insisting that the child be adopted as soon as it was born. Clodagh immediately said she wanted to raise him.

Your mother was hostile to the idea of her taking William to begin with. When Clodagh threatened to get the authorities involved they struck a rather unsavoury agreement. These days that would simply not happen. Clodagh Anchorage was told that you had rejected your baby and so a new mother was being sought outside of Trellinick.

Violet agreed that Clodagh could have the baby, but she was to leave Trellinick forever and never tell anyone who the real mother was. She made her swear never to contact you or reveal to you that she had your son. So desperate was she to keep her grandson and not have him sent to live with an unknown family, lost to them all, she agreed. A contract was drawn up by the vicar and signed by both women. A contract with absolutely no legal standing but with all due respect to these ladies, they wouldn't have known that."

Marjorie sobbed quietly. "She was evil. Pure evil." Hetty had her arm around her - both of them trying to make sense of what they were hearing.

"But what about Michael? Surely Michael knew? Why did he never contact me?"

"He was never told the baby was his. Let me read the letter to you, Marjorie, it will all make sense to you then."

"This is all too much, Harry, I cannot believe it. My boy was with his family this whole time and I didn't know. My mother told me he was in Norfolk. She said a suitable family had been found and he was taken to Norfolk. How could she be so cruel? Until her death she kept it from me. How could she?"

"Would you like a break, Marjorie? I can wait. This is a

massive discovery, I know that. I managed to find the adoption papers after a lot of searching but it's true, he stayed with his own family where he belonged. Would you like me to read the letter? Or would you rather take it away with you and read it later when you are alone?"

"No, I would like you to read it if you could please, Harry. I need to hear it, and I want Hetty to hear it too. She took hold of her hands, squeezing them tightly. Finishing my coffee, I lifted the letter and read.

My darling Marjorie,

How will you ever forgive me? Maybe you never will and maybe I should never expect forgiveness. Perhaps I should just hope for understanding. I want you to know that I loved your son dearly and still do. Despite your mother insisting I change his name, I held as part of this unsavoury bargain, that whichever name you chose, your son will thusly be named. So, he was and will always be 'William'. By the time you receive this letter, Michael will know who William really is to him.

You see, I agreed with your mother that I would not tell Michael the baby was his. He had no knowledge of your pregnancy as he had left Trellinick. I'm sure it was before you would even have known yourself. I struck so many bargains in order to keep your son safely with me, it was like dancing with the devil. To that end however, I did as I promised and told Michael that I was adopting the baby as his mother had passed in childbirth and the baby was quite alone in the world. Please forgive me for that too, if you can.

I signed the papers presented to me by the vicar with clear instructions. I left Trellinick when William was given to me by your mother when he was just ten days old. She handed him to me in a small blanket and gave me nothing more by way of possessions. No pram, no clothes, no toys. Just an innocent infant sleeping as if to hide from this deceit. A heartless plot to secrete him away. Understanding he would be coming to me, I had bought him some tiny clothes already and other essentials, but she gave me nothing to signify the love and excitement a family feels at the arrival of a new baby. I knew how you would likely be hurting Marjorie, but your mother insisted you had rejected the baby so wanted no personal effects for him. I couldn't bear the thought of my grandson being placed with strangers. He was my flesh and blood and whilst it was clear he had one unloving grandmother; he certainly did not have two.

With Michael in Exeter, I rented a house there to start with. The one decent thing your mother did in all of this Marjorie was to leave me money for his care. I initially had no desire to take the money from her; William was not an item to have a price attached to. It meant however, I could leave immediately. I had promised her that on the day William was placed into my care that I would leave. I was so afraid your mother would change her mind, that I stuck religiously to the terms of our arrangement. At that time, Michael was living in a small bedsit in Exeter, and I wanted to be near him. Of course, I also wanted William to be with his father, albeit I could never reveal that father and son was actually the nature of their relationship.

You must try to understand Marjorie, these were very different times. This could never happen now, no doubt, but back then, these kinds of arrangements were common enough. Michael adored William and though he thought of him as his baby brother, they very quickly forged a strong bond with each other. Once I had sold my home in Trellinick, I bought a house in Exeter and the three of us lived together, which worked out just fine. I stopped working and took full-time care of William. Michael continued to impress and worked very hard and sat all kinds of exams and qualifications in accountancy. I don't even know the name of them all. He is now the Director of Finance for a large manufacturing company and is still living in Exeter. He retires very soon.

I told William that I wasn't his real mummy before he started primary school. I felt as innocent as he was, he had the right to know that at least. I was desperate to tell him I was his grandmother, but of course I couldn't as that would mean Michael would know he was his father. It was so unbearably complicated. Like children often do, William took the news calmly and was very matter of fact about it. He simply remarked that mummies were kind ladies who looked after children and as I was one of those ladies, to him I was his mummy and that was that.

He occasionally would make a reference to his 'real mother's family' but so content was he with our little set up, I don't think it occurred to him to actively seek out his birth family.

When William was twelve, Michael and his partner Moira, who was a nurse, were married and William was best man. It was such a memorable day, and I secretly wished then, as I do now, that you had been there to see your handsome son standing at the altar, best man to his father. I stayed in the house after they married and Michael and Moira lived very close by, so we continued to see a lot of each other. They had their first child Evie two years after they married, quickly followed by Joey just over a year after that. Michael was a natural father but of course, I already knew that.

Only the Lonely

Your amazing son William was such a smart boy and did very well at school. He stayed at home with me until he went to university to study Architecture at Bath University. He was so career minded I thought he wouldn't marry. Destined to be a bachelor I thought. He worked his way through the ranks of a few architectural firms until he opened his own practice when he was thirty-four. It quickly grew; his reputation was so good. It was while he was working on a big project in Exeter that he met Sofia. She was working as a surveyor on the project, and they evidently hit it off straight away. They were married two years later and have a new young son called Oscar who is the love of my life. So that makes you a grandmother, Marjorie. He was born on 1st February 2016 and was the greatest present anyone could wish for. I'm thrilled to let you know baby number two is on the way too.

Michael's life however took a dreadful turn six years ago when Moira discovered a lump in her breast which turned out to be cancer. She battled very hard, bless her soul, but sadly she passed, and Michael has been alone since. He is very stoic about it all, because that's his way and Evie and Joey have been an enormous comfort to him, but I know he misses Moira terribly, which is totally understandable.

I cannot even guess how he will take the news I am about to give him. Michael is such an incredible son, I imagine he will understand that I had no other choice. You see Marjorie, once you find yourself caught in a web of lies, it is so difficult to escape from it, to know how to escape from it. I think your chappy Harry has given me the way out.

Only the Lonely

When your investigating man arrived at the home to say he was trying to find William, I was so happy Marjorie. Probably the happiest I have been in years. Actually, I don't think I mean happy, I think I mean relieved. You see, holding on to secrets that aren't yours to hold is wearing.

Marjorie, I am eighty-four years old now and I have no idea how long I have left, though I am not planning on going any time soon. I want you to know that I have loved and cherished every day I spent with your son William. I know I am his grandmother, but I can see the crime here was that you, his mother, was robbed of the chance to love him, to know him and to raise him.

I hope you know that I will always carry that guilt but that I did everything I could to give your son the best possible life in a home where he was loved and cherished. I would love to meet you Marjorie and explain all this in person. I will leave that decision to you but know that I would welcome you here with open arms.

I pray that Michael is understanding when I tell him his real relationship to William, and of course William likewise, but any fallout it creates I deserve for holding this secret for so long. I have held onto this heart-breaking secret Marjorie and at times it has tormented me. Harry has told me that your mother has passed now but she was at the centre of it all. I will not speak ill of the dead Marjorie, but what happened to you and as a result to Michael and William was so very wrong. Today however as I write this letter to you, I feel lighter. Truth brings comfort and releases the weight and burden of deceitfulness. I am not a bad person, and I pray you see that. I will never regret the blessing William was to our families, but I will always regret that you

Only the Lonely

were missing from his life.

I will be here Marjorie,

Clodagh Anchorage.

I gently folded the letter up and placed it back in the envelope. I looked from Marjorie to Hetty but said nothing. We sat in silence as the minutes passed with the noises of a busy café for company. The waitress who had served us our drinks returned with a fresh tray and placed it on the table.

"Let me take these cups away from you and here's some fresh tea and coffee. You all look like you could use some warm drinks. There will be no charge."

Hetty looked at her and mouthed her thanks to the waitress and took hold of Marjorie's hand.

"My goodness, Marjorie, what a story. Is it simply too soon to ask you how you feel?"

"I don't know, Hetty. I honestly don't know how I feel. I'm elated and frightened and angry and confused. All this 'normal life' was happening just seventy miles from me, and I had no idea."

I then placed a card in front of Marjorie, "You do not have to do anything Marjorie, but this is a lady I work closely with who specialises in helping my clients come to terms with news like this. This has been a mind-blowing journey for you. You haven't just found your son, but you now know you have a grandson called Oscar. That is a lot for anyone to take in."

Marjorie picked the card up and stared at it. She ran the edge of the card across her fingers, not daring to look up as tears fell onto the table. First one, then another, then another, then rapidly more. Hetty tearfully held her friend as they gathered themselves.

"Harry, I don't know how to thank you. I don't know the words. What you have done has given me a purpose. I swore to my boy William as he was taken from my arms that one day I would find him. That he would know I loved him and now that can happen. I pray it will be what he wants. I want to look into my grandson's eyes, as Clodagh did with her grandson, and tell him I love him too.

Thank you for finding my son. Thank you for uncovering the truth. Thank you for giving me my title back. I am a mother again. What happens now Harry?"

I took a deep breath and then whilst I held onto Marjorie's hand I looked at them both.

"Right now, we do nothing. We sit here in Harrods, having tea with Audrey Hepburn. Then in a week, in a month, in six months, whenever you're ready Marjorie we do whatever you want."

CHAPTER FORTY-ONE
Marjorie

We left Harrod's and said our good-byes to Harry. He assured me that he would be in touch but if I wanted to reach out to him, I could. Hetty and I decided to walk slowly back to the hotel. Take stock. Hetty was unusually quiet which unnerved me somewhat. She smiled at me when I looked across at her and just quietly spoke.

"Marjorie I don't quite know what to say. I cannot begin to imagine how you must feel. It's great news that William is alive and well and was raised by his own family. I just can't believe your mother's role in this whole deception. How on earth could she have done that to you. I just don't get it. Seventy miles away. That's all he ever was, seventy miles."

"I know. I feel both heart broken and elated. My head is mashed. Am I right to feel a bit angry towards Clodagh for not reaching out to me Hetty? Fine, she couldn't when William was a child, but why not once he was an adult?"

"Marjorie of course you're entitled to feel every emotion simmering just now. I can only think that Clodagh was so damaged or frightened by what your mother and that Vicar threatened her with that she just let things continue. She said they happy little family unit, perhaps she just didn't want to upset the apple cart. I don't know Marj. It's so horribly complicated."

"I'm worried how William will react when he finds out his adopted brother is actually his biological father - and that's just the first part. He also needs to grapple with the fact that Clodagh is not his adopted mother; she's his biological grandmother."

"You couldn't make this up Marjorie. You really couldn't. So many lives affected and the two people at the centre of it, you and Michael left totally in the dark. William was your baby. It just seems so crazy that this could have happened. Here you go Clodagh, there's some money and a baby. Now off you go. How could your mother even look at herself in the mirror?

Sorry Marjorie, I know she was your mother, but she was one hateful, selfish bitch."

"Perfectly put Hetty. Please do not apologise. I can't find words to describe my hatred for her."

We carried on walking. People breezing and pushing past us as we silently tried to process what we had just learnt. It was my news, but I knew Hetty felt it profoundly too. She had been with me since I announced that I was pregnant, through to the morning William was stolen and beyond. A constant at my side. I couldn't have wanted anyone else with me. Hetty was the flesh and blood my mother never was to me.

I knew what I'd read in her journal. I didn't care. It was no excuse. Maybe this was the ultimate way for Violet to punish me for my very existence.

'*I sat up at night and mourned the life I never got to live.*'

That's what she'd written. Pitying herself whilst inflicting the very same pain on me. How dare she decide that having a baby would be history repeating itself. She knew I wanted William, that I loved him and was willing to give my life to him. Yet she selfishly took that away from me. That was a cruelty I will never recover from.

Back at the hotel, we checked out and waited as our doormen friends hailed us a cab for the station. We put on brave faces and joked with them about this now being an annual event and we'd look forward to seeing them next year. I really had taken a shine to them.

Hetty mysteriously disappeared back inside whilst we waited and had a very mischievous grin on her face when she returned. She assured me it was not Brodie related but I didn't mind regardless. I was relieved to see her smile again. The weight of what Harry had told us had knocked the wind out of our sails.

I knew I should probably have been jumping through hoops. My search was over. My son was discovered. There was a hope we could be reunited. Yet my mind was tangled. This wasn't as simple as a child returning from university who you've missed for three months. My child had a life of his own. He knew nothing of my existence. He believed me to be dead. Neither did he know the true identity of the people who had cared for him all his life. No, I would need to tread very carefully and thoughtfully before making any movements towards William and Exeter. This was an apple cart I would have to upset very slowly.

I knew who we needed to talk to.

Albert.

CHAPTER FORTY-TWO
Hetty

We retrieved our suitcases from the left luggage room by reception and took a seat whilst a taxi was organised.

"Well bloody hell, Marjorie Hepburn. I defy anyone to call you boring. What on earth happened today? Breakfast at Tiffany's followed by the most incredible story of how your son was raised. Not by some random family in Norfolk, but by his own father and grandmother, and all that by the way, without his father's knowledge. Crazy just crazy."

I remember holding her. We held back our tears. The last thing Marjorie would have wanted was for people to see her distress. We both agreed, we needed to get home to Beachcombers and Albert.

We walked back outside and said our final goodbyes to the two delightful doormen. They probably loved every guest, but I allowed myself the luxury of believing we were superspecial guests.

As we clambered into the taxi Marjorie placed a quantity of notes into their gloved hands, and we set off for Paddington station. When we arrived in the concourse, Marjorie insisted that even though we were now somewhat laden with suitcases, handbags and a whirl of emotions, that we grab a coffee from Starbucks one last time. It really made me smile but I was more than happy to go along with it. I'm sure it was just so that we 'fitted in' with the other travellers and made us appear to be well-seasoned train commuters.

We stayed on the concourse amid the clatter of noises from trollies and suitcases and platform announcements and sipped our respective beverages. When the tannoy announced that the train for Truro was at platform six, a gentle swathe of fellow passengers moved towards the platform. We boarded the train and once again took our seats in the first-class compartment for our last experience of luxury. We were aware of the array of technology being plugged in, switched on and typed into. We put our bags in the compartment above our seats, together with our coats, and settled in for the long journey. Marjorie then checked her phone.

Hi Marjorie, I just wanted to check you got your train alright. It was a pleasure to meet you and Hetty. I hope sincerely as the news sinks in that you can enjoy it and feel comforted knowing where William is. I will organise the next steps once you're ready – not before. I look forward to hearing all the details of your reunion in Trellinick with Albert. Take care of yourself. Harry

I also checked my own phone. My little heart skipped a beat as there, in my inbox, were two messages from Brodie. I'm sure I went a little red. Marjorie looked up at me and said, "I take it you've had a text from Brodie, Missy. You certainly don't smile like that or go as red as you are when I text you." I giggled and confirmed that I had heard from him and that he was just interested in how today had gone. We smiled at each other and clinked our paper coffee cups in a mock toast to new beginnings.

As the train trundled out of the station, the waitress arrived to take our order for drinks and what we would like from the food menu. In the past few days, I felt like I had both eaten and drunk enough to last a lifetime, but just to be polite I ordered a chilled white wine and a selection of sandwiches together with a side salad and a chocolate brownie for dessert. As Marjorie was busily typing her response to Harry, I ordered the same for her too. Once Marjorie pressed 'send' on her message, she put the phone down on the table and sighed deeply.

"Oh Hetty, I'm a mother again and for keeps this time. I'm so excited. Do you think Michael would have taken the news well? What a thing to be told out of the blue. That your childhood sweetheart and you made a baby together and that Evie and Joey actually have a brother in William. What will William make of it all. My poor boy."

"You know Marjorie, our minds are a whirl with all this. No doubt theirs will be too. We all need to take stock. You've waited this long to see William again, perhaps a few more weeks or months, if that's what it takes, is the price to be paid to give them time to process. To be fair Marjorie, you need to take stock too."

I was so struck when Marjorie questioned why Clodagh hadn't reached out sooner. I privately questioned that too. Surely, she knew she still lived alone in Trellinick. I would keep my thoughts to myself, however. This was certainly not the time for recriminations.

The waitress arrived with our food and drinks and Marjorie looked somewhat shocked by the amount of food I had appeared to order. We tucked in nonetheless and chatted about our trip.

"What a trip Hetty. I keep pinching myself to ensure it really happened. Besides the information from Harry, what were your highlights? Or actually I guess I should be asking you who was your highlight, you little minx?'

"I know, I'm a little excited, you know. I actually can't believe I met Brodie. He seems like a genuinely nice man. Let's be honest, any man would feel like an upgrade after what Edwin put me through in end. Anyway, the main highlight has obviously been finding out about William. It's hard to pick out another favourite bit, honestly, it's all been so memorable. Harry was a really nice bloke, wasn't he? Seeing your face as we entered the café at Harrods was priceless, us having breakfast at Tiffany's with your Audrey Hepburn after a lifetime of waiting. The argument at the wine bar, ah Marjorie, do you remember that? Those women were hilarious. Naughty old Phee! Christ, I hope she wasn't married to a man called Brodie who went home and whispered my name to his wife as they made sweet nothings. Could you imagine?"

"You didn't sleep with him did you Hetty? You didn't sneak him up to your room did you?"

"No, no. Of course not. Christ Marjorie, how would I have explained Brodie to Colin Firth. Right, enough about Brodie - what about you, honey, what have you enjoyed, besides today obviously?"

"Do you know what, Hetty, I totally enjoyed every second because I spent it with you. I'm not just being corny, Hetty, seeing the joy on your face during every step of this trip was the pleasure I found in it. There isn't a single bit of this trip I wouldn't do again. I even enjoyed that cheeky detour to Ann Summers. Alan Titchmarsh has introduced me to parts of my body I didn't know existed Hetty. He's such a considerate lover. He's there in my bag, wrapped up in my scarf to muffle the noise in case he goes off!"

We then properly laughed. Out loud and boisterous. The laughter of two women with the cheekiest of secrets.

"Isn't it just amazing that we found each other, Marjorie? Life has thrown so much at us both but because we had each other, we got through it. At your loneliest points I was there for you and you for me. You were there for me during my darkest days with Edwin and I will always be so grateful. From marriage to his tragic death, you were there. I was there for you too during your pregnancy and the day your mother took William away. I feel so privileged to be a part of any potential reunion.

It's also amazing that we found Albert, the third lonely soul in our story. I have a feeling life might be changing for him too. I've seen a softening in his face when he mentions Kathleen. I can't put my finger on it, but it's there."

With that thought ringing in our ears, for the umpteenth time on the trip, we clinked glasses and downed our wine before ordering two more. We then continued to chatter and giggle about our few days away and relished the thought that we would be seeing our darling friend

Only the Lonely

Albert in just a few hours too. Not long after our second glasses of wine were emptied, with flushed cheeks and safely stored memories, we both drifted off to sleep.

Hours and several trips to the ladies later, we pulled into Truro train station. We were both so excited to see Albert and debated which timepiece collecting us would demand of him. We gathered our bags and coats and joined the queue of people waiting to leave the train. I turned and gave Marjorie another long and deep hug for giving me the most unbelievable few days away. She whispered it had been her pleasure and thank goodness for discarded cash on morning walks. We smiled conspiratorially at each other and giggled at the enormity of it all.

We left the train, laden with bags and gifts and then we spotted Albert. With two bunches of beautiful roses, he waved frantically at us and mouthed, 'welcome home'. My guess of a waistcoat and gold pocket watch was clearly correct. He was just the quintessential example of an English gentleman. I rushed into his arms as he presented me with the flowers and did likewise with Marjorie.

"Well, my gorgeous girls. You decided to come home after all. I am so thrilled I haven't lost you both to the lure of the bright lights and fancy dining! I simply cannot wait to hear all about your trip. I loved the photographs by the way; they really made me chuckle. I deleted the rather revealing ones you sent Hetty! The place has been so quiet without you both. Well, without you Hetty.'

He insisted on taking our loose shopping bags as we made our way to his car. 'I bet you've got plenty to tell me.'

"Oh Albert, you have no idea. We have literally so much to tell you."

"Well, I suspected as much so I have bought Battenberg cake. Sorry, Marjorie, I didn't make it. How about I get you ladies home, and we meet at mine for a morning debrief? You must both be exhausted."

"Of course, can it be PJ's though, Marjorie? I just want to be in my casuals again."

"Do you honestly think I am wandering around in my nightie, Hetty? Really? How well do you actually know me? I will bring my nightclothes to your home, Albert, and change once I'm there, if that is alright with you."

"Yes, Marjorie, that will do nicely. Oh, my goodness, but I've missed you two."

I arrived back at Albert's at ten in the morning and was quite happily sipping tea in my tartan pyjamas as 'Lady Marjorie' arrived, fully dressed, wheeling a large suitcase which she described as an overnight bag! Unbelievable! She then disappeared into Albert's guest room and reappeared minutes later wrapped up in a white fluffy Savoy Hotel dressing gown which had been embossed with her name. She then presented me with one and handed a second over to Albert. I leapt from my seat and rushed to her. She also gave us our own Savoy Hotel slippers."

"Oh, my goodness, Marjorie, how have you done that? Wow, it's got my name on it and yours does too, Albert! The surprises just keep coming, this is amazing. Thank you Marjorie, thank you so very much."

"We were in London Hetty and at The Savoy. One word with the concierge and the dressing gowns were sent off to be printed and returned the same day. You simply ask and they make it happen."

Albert stood admiring himself in his wall mounted mirror, "Well yes, customer service is no doubt they're buzz word. Look at me in my Savoy dressing gown. How terribly decadent is this? I look quite the sight, don't I?"

"You do, Albert, you look very dapper. Now Marjorie, the floor is all yours. Let's tell our gorgeous friend about our trip while we sip tea and polish of this Battenberg."

I curled into Albert as Marjorie sat opposite us. Looking like the chair of a meeting she recounted the story.

We listened.

We cried.

We laughed.

But the three of us were together again.

CHAPTER FORTY-THREE
Albert

It had been so quiet without my girls and the rhythm and interest they brought to my life. For three days I had the company of my darling Emily but after she left to return to work, I realised just how much I had grown to rely on my lady friends for company.

Marjorie had, of course, asked the other couples on the Beachcombers to keep an eye out for me, which was both adorable and unnecessary.

When Emily arrived back home I chatted with her for an hour or so on FaceTime, which was marvellous. She and her partner Stefan were in the middle of moving house to Solihull in the West Midlands to start their own legal practice. Stefan had been there for years and had a number of contacts, and the commute was killing them both, so the move was being made.

I couldn't be prouder of my girl. She had recovered so well from her illness and, while a constant eye would now always be kept on her, she was as healthy as the rest of us. Though I never said it, I wished Kathleen, and I could go together to view Emily and Stefan's new house. I was the one being stubborn, I knew that. I just couldn't find the way or the words to break free of my own dogged resolve to maintain the distance. Kathleen had hurt me terribly but if Emily could forgive her, surely it was time I did.

As Marjorie left my home late in the afternoon, following their return from London, Hetty and I opened a bottle of wine and sat back down for a good old catch-up, which we often did. After a more candid description of the trip away, which included their trip to the Ann Summers adult shop (hilarious - I simply cannot picture Marjorie in there). She also told me about her flirtation with this gentleman Brodie. She seems quite taken.

The chatter then turned to Kathleen and my move to Beachcombers.

"How did you come to be here, Albert? I mean I know what happened with Kathleen and I remember we met at the Pensbury's marketing night when we learnt about this place. But why here, how did that happen?"

I hadn't realised that I had not previously explained the story to my friends, in any great detail. I suppose I'm just rather more reserved than Hetty is at least, and Marjorie's story and her search for William was definitely an open story. It hadn't been a subject that had ever been broached before. I guessed now that Marjorie had discovered William, the time was right to tell my story. Life was moving on and now just might be the time to bare my soul.

"The day I found out Kathleen had slept with Charlie, though it was a crushing blow, I knew I still loved her, Hetty. In fact, I still do now. In spite of the years and the obvious damage, I love her so much my heart hurts. When she told me that Emily wasn't mine, no, when I discovered Emily wasn't mine from her specialist, I just couldn't believe it. To discover that the person you loved and believed in could lie about something as precious as a child, I just couldn't find a way to forgive her. I tried to, believe me I tried to, but I just couldn't. Love was pushing me towards her but the hurt in knowing what she did was pushing me away.

As I look back now, I'm not sure which part of this whole mess was driving my emotions. Was it that Emily wasn't my child, though I knew I loved her just the same. Was it that my wife had been unfaithful with Charlie of all people? I was really tormented by it. I couldn't get the image of the two of them giggling playfully at Harvey's youngest daughters christening. Holding candles and praying to their God, the perfect facsimile of Christian Godparents. Yet little did I know they were so much more than Godparents, they were Emily's parents. I really couldn't bear it.

Only the Lonely

The days and weeks after we told Emily were excruciating. Kathleen tried her best to be her usual loving self around me. Emily was also particularly cuddly with me and attentive. It was as if she wanted to reassure me that nothing had changed, she did still think of me as her father.

But you see, Hetty, it was all so fake. It was beyond uncomfortable to be there. I was civil with Kathleen, and we attended several social functions together and I knew that although Emily had returned to university, she kept in constant contact with her mother to ensure we were doing alright. But the simple truth was that we were not doing alright. I slept in the guest room and, though we dined together on the evenings Kathleen was home, we pretty much lived apart albeit in the same house.

After about two months of this charade, I contacted Milly and asked if she knew of a good hotel or B&B that I could stay in on the coast so I could just get away for a while and clear my mind. She invited me to stay with them here but at their house, not in a B&B. This site was all just disused farmland at the time. They had these fabulous plans for the land though. While I was down here, they organised the open evening where I met you and Marjorie for the first time. It was never my intention to come here permanently.

My intention was to rent this home for an initial period of six months, which could be extended should I wish. But when I returned home to Surrey after my brief trip down here, Kathleen was waiting for me in the kitchen. It was clear she wasn't coping either. She broke down, Hetty. Totally broke down into my arms. I knew our marriage was over and so did she, but I wanted so desperately to make it right again. The chasm her lies had generated though was simply too big. Neither of us was able to put it somewhere and carry on. I knew counselling wouldn't work. The truth of what Kathleen had done could not be erased by a third party.

I can see it now though. I can see the truth of her actions and I forgive her."

"Then do something, Albert, tell her. Tell her you forgive her. Don't let her go again, Albert. If your heart is where it needs to be to get over this, then tell her honey, please Albert. Did she meet someone else? Please tell me she didn't get with that Charlie?"

"No, she didn't get with Charlie. That's another twist. The tragedy continued, Hetty. Charlie was tragically killed in a car crash, ironically down here somewhere. So, no she didn't continue a relationship with him but honestly I don't think that was ever on the cards. I'm not even sure if he knew he was Emily's father. I think he did, she had at least told him she was pregnant and just weeks after they had slept together. There's no sense in dwelling on something I will never know now.

Time doesn't heal your wounds; it simply allows your heart space to grow around whatever consumes you and kneads it until it softens so you can simply carry on. You can never heal from news like this. It's too permanent. But I've learnt as I'm getting older that life doesn't come wrapped in neat packages of events that can be opened to produce a predictable outcome. It's full of twists and turns and you have to adapt or fall. It's as simple as that. You and Marjorie know that better than anyone.

I know Kathleen has moved on with her life. She still lives in our home, and I wish her nothing but happiness, but I honestly wouldn't know how to reach out to her now, Hetty. It's been too long, and I can't assume that just because I'm ready to forgive her, that she would welcome me back into her life anyway."

"But what if she did, Albert? What if she's sitting at home tonight thinking about you and wondering if you could ever forgive her?"

"If only I had your confidence Hetty. Charlie McBride took more than fatherhood from me. He took my confidence and my belief in humanity."

"Charlie McBride? Was that his name, Albert? Oh my God. Albert, oh my God. You are not going to believe this."

"What Hetty, what's wrong?"

"The man Edwin killed that night in Padstow, the car he hit, was driven by a Charlie McBride. It couldn't be the same man, could it? Let me get my laptop and let's look on the internet. When was Charlie killed Albert, can you remember?"

Only the Lonely

Hetty was frantically uploading Google and typing in Edwin's name together with Charlie McBride. As I stared into space trying to think of the date, she looked up at me and froze.

"Well, I'd struggle for the actual date, but it would have been in 2008. This is too weird Hetty, it can't be the same man."

"Christ alive Albert it is. You're right, this is too weird. Look. Charlie McBride from Edinburgh was killed in a tragic accident caused by a drunk driver on the A3059 from Padstow on the night of Friday 20th June 2008. Edwin killed him, Albert. Oh my goodness. I am so sorry. This is just unbelievable. I don't know what to say."

I took the laptop from Hetty and read the article, shaking my head as I did so. Every few seconds whispering 'unbelievable'.

"What the heck was Charlie McBride doing on the road out of Padstow on the night my stupidly drunk husband stole a car and forced him off the road killing him? Ten years we have lived here with you, Albert. Ten years and it took me trying to persuade you to forgive Kathleen to reveal this terrible coincidence. We almost went to his funeral you know. I felt so horrible about what Edwin had done.

I wondered if I shouldn't go to pay my respects, but it was in Edinburgh I had the children and Marjorie persuaded me I probably wouldn't be welcome anyway. I would have seen you, wouldn't I? I'm guessing you went?"

"Yes, I went out of respect for Harvey. At the time he was killed, I knew little of his life really. Outside of our social gatherings at Harvey and Morag's house I wouldn't exactly say we were chummy. He didn't come to Harvey's that often once he married Agnes, and they had baby Isla. As I recall though, his wife's family lived in Newlyn so maybe he had been visiting them for some reason. Perhaps they had been in Padstow for the day. I didn't quiz Harvey about it at the time. He was naturally shocked, and no doubt devastated, Charlie was his only sibling. Harvey came to Cornwall to formally identify his brother and escort his body back to Edinburgh where his funeral took place. I was there but for what I now know were obvious reasons, Kathleen was not."

I simply shook my head. "Honestly Albert, if all of this wasn't happening here, to us, I wouldn't believe it could happen in real life. How can it be that you and I are now linked by this terrible tragedy?"

"Well, it happened a long time ago now Hetty and I've shed enough tears for Charlie McBride. Not just at his passing but for what he took from me. I'm not about to let him come between us now. Edwin did this not you. Don't carry Edwin's guilt sweetheart, believe me carrying the wrongs of other people is draining."

"Do you think Harvey knew Albert? Do you think Charlie ever told Harvey he'd slept with Kathleen and ultimately could be the father of her baby?"

"Hetty there isn't a doubt in my mind that he knew. They moved away shortly after Emily was born and we stopped socialising with them almost completely. Initially I just put it down to child commitments. They had three children in the end, and I don't doubt the children did take up most of their time. In truth though, Harvey and Charlie were thick as thieves so of course he knew. You know the hardest thing of all Hetty, Emily looks like him. I can see Charlie in her. She obviously looks like Kathleen too. But I can also see Harvey. I hadn't seen it until I found the truth of her parentage, but once I knew, I couldn't not see it. At times, when I'm thinking of it all, I see I wasn't just deceived by Kathleen, I was deceived by the three of them. The worst kind of love triangle.'

"Christ. What about Morag? Do you think she knew?"

"No, I don't think so. She was so supportive when all this broke with Emily. First her illness then who her father was. She was too genuine to be faking her shock and sympathy. So no, another lie Harvey lived with, I don't think he told Morag before it all broke."

I walked over to Albert and put my arms around his shoulders. 'Albert, I genuinely don't know what to say. I cannot believe this bond we now have. My DNA runs through Marjorie's veins as hers does mine. But now I discover, for such tragic reasons, yours does too. How can one little slice of Cornish shoreline throw up such incredible stories. William, the money, London, and now this. This won't change us will it, Albert? We'll still be us, won't we?"

I took her hands in mine and for the first time since moving to Beachcombers, I cried. 'That man took the only relationship I ever truly cared about and wrecked it. He stole my belief in humanity and the power of true love and true friendship. In you and Marjorie, I found it again. A different version but nonetheless, the power of true friendship. You must never worry that I would let him take that from me a second time, Hetty. So, believe me when I say nothing will ever change what we have here.

Maybe it's time, as I grow older, to forgive Kathleen, but I will never forget or forgive what Charlie did to me and my family in life, so I won't let him come between us in death."

"What about Harvey though, Albert? You can't blame him for the actions of his brother. If he did know, then it was his brother who put him in an impossible position. Harvey was stuck in the middle Albert. If he didn't know, then again, he's innocent in all of this. It seems from everything you've told Marjorie and I, you four had a real friendship. I think you have some real hatchet burying to do my friend. Just think about it anyway."

Hetty stayed with me until I was able to compose myself and process the enormity of the news we had just uncovered. She was right I knew that. I had held such a grudge against Harvey when he'd actually done nothing wrong. It was still hard to reconcile that he was a blood relation of Emily's, and I was not. I needed to stop wallowing in self-pity about that, silly, stubborn old fool that I was. I was cross with myself for getting upset.

Hetty was her marvellous self however and made no big deal of it. As I walked her home the few steps to her door, I kissed her forehead and she said one more time, "Do you think you could forgive Kathleen and Harvey and slowly allow them back into your life, Albert? I'm sure Emily would love that. It must be so hard on Emily when she loves you both so much. Life's too short Albie. Surely Marjorie has proved that these last few weeks.

Sleep well soul mate. We are inexorably linked my Albert Hargraves."

I smiled and hugged her so hard I feared she would pop. 'Yes agreed, life is too darn short. Do you know, I always knew we had an extra special friendship, Hetty. I just didn't know why until this evening. Maybe I should swallow my pride and reach out to them both. A fear of rejection frightens the hardiest of us. I wish I was as brave as you. Sleep well soul mate and welcome home."

I walked back inside and locked my door.

Now Kathleen. What do I do next?

Part Three

William

CHAPTER FORTY-FOUR
William

I had never questioned the importance of family until events in my life occurred to make me think about it more deeply. I had grown up in such a loving home with Clodagh Anchorage, the woman who had adopted me when I was just weeks old. I had one brother, Michael, over twenty years my senior but with whom I have always enjoyed the strongest of bonds.

We lived in a small semi-detached house in Exeter and life, though challenging at times, was happy and I felt lucky to have been adopted by such a loving, attentive lady. Clodagh Anchorage was not my mother, but she was the perfect facsimile of one and that had always been good enough for me. I had been told that my mother had died shortly after my birth, so I had no desire to contact my extended biological family. As far as I was concerned, Clodagh and Michael were my family.

When I was twelve years old my brother married and left us, to buy his own home with his new wife Moira. Though they still lived very close by, I felt I became an even bigger part of my mother's world. Even as a grandchild arrived shortly after my brother's marriage, my mother still doted on me and ensured I remained her primary focus.

However, years passed, and with the unwavering encouragement I received from my mother, I went off to Bath University.

I left university with my degree in Architecture and started my first job at a local architectural practice in Bath. I moved to a few different practices in the southwest before gaining what I considered were enough stripes to set up my own practice. I was committed to my work and although I had embarked on a few casual relationships, nothing too serious had ever blossomed so I felt as I reached my mid-thirties that I would remain a bachelor. That was not destined to remain the case however. Whilst working on a project just outside Exeter, I met Sofia. She stole my heart completely. Our relationship developed very quickly and within two years we were married. I was thrilled that in the year I turned forty, we welcomed our son Oscar Anchorage. Life seemed settled and perfect.

However, that changed somewhat a few months ago when my mother announced she was finding the family home too much to maintain. At eighty-four, she would be happier in residential care rather than trying to run the house alone. Despite mine and Michael's best efforts to have her come and live with one of us, she was adamant she didn't want to be a burden and would rather be in a home with her peers and on-site medical care. She'd had one fall in the garden and whilst it wasn't serious, it had knocked her confidence. In the end we relented.

Michael and I were both saddened by our mother's decision but, ever a lady who knew her own mind, we agreed with her and set the wheels in motion. When we found a home that she loved and where we thought she would receive the first-rate care she deserved, she moved in. Soon after her move, however, I felt she aged. She seemed to take on the appearance of an older lady rather than the vibrant, energetic woman I had always clung to believing her to be. She was certainly happy there and had spared no time in making new friends, it's just that I now saw her growing frail and less independent.

What my mother didn't know, however, was that shortly after she had moved into her care home, I had discovered who my real mother was. I had decided not to tell her. I didn't want to do anything to cause her pain or leave her feeling that in some way she hadn't been enough of a mother to me. Having found out however, I just felt a longing to meet my birth mother. A mother I had been told had passed away.

Ironically it was Clodagh herself who inadvertently planted that seed in me. One evening just before her moving date, she left the room and returned, handing Sofia and I a cheque for one hundred thousand pounds. She explained that when I was handed over to her, my mother's family had also given her a sum of money for my care. They maintained they were not in a position to raise me themselves but would financially contribute towards my care. We both doubted they had actually given such a large amount of money, but Clodagh was adamant. She had used a small amount of it to enable her to move with me to Exeter, but the rest she had put in trust for when I needed it. She'd decided to give me the money now, before she moved to her care home and in order that we could use it to prepare for the new baby. We were naturally shocked by just how savvy Clodagh had been.

As we walked home that evening, I stared at the cheque and for the first time in my life, I felt a connection to my birth family. This was the first gesture I had ever been aware of from them. Suddenly they had become real to me, and I wanted to know more about them. Sofia initially tried to persuade me that it was a mistake. What if they rejected me? She pointed out my mother had died, and I had no idea who my father was. But whatever it was that was driving me, I needed to know who they were. I think the fact that I had known the joy of becoming a father myself was also driving this need in me.

I firstly asked Michael what he knew of my mother. He just shook his head and reassured me he knew as much as I did; he seemed to remember his mother saying that my birth mother had died in childbirth, but he could be misremembering. However, as we cleared her house just after Clodagh had moved, I found a box in her wardrobe containing the answers I sought. My mother had not died, or at least not in childbirth.

The box contained a number of letters and papers relating to the house purchase, her husband's death certificate, birth certificates and lots of my achievement certificates from school, swimming club, cubs, and scouts. However, towards the bottom was a typed, rather unofficial-looking agreement, signed and dated just after my birth between my adoptive mother, Clodagh Anchorage, and a Marjorie Hepburn, my birth mother.

So, Marjorie Hepburn was my mother.

The bigger shock was who my real father was.

Michael Anchorage.

I was totally stunned. Clodagh was my grandmother, and Michael was not my brother but was, in fact, my father. I sat on the bed in stunned silence and read the agreement:

Agreement for the care of the infant:

William Hepburn official name Anchorage

This agreement has been entered into freely and is agreed upon by both parties. The infant from now on known as William Michael Anchorage will be given over to the care of:

Name: *Clodagh Anchorage*

Date: *22nd April 1972*

Address: *Applegarth, High Street, Trellinick, North Cornwall, PL28 2NA*

Only the Lonely

From the care of:

Name: *Marjorie May Hepburn*

Date: *22nd April 1972*

Address: *36, Peach Blossom Lane, Trellinick, North Cornwall, PL28 2PA*

Clodagh Anchorage agrees to leave Trellinick with William and not reside back in the village or the surrounding area, for as long as William remains in her care. Once he has grown and left home, she will be free to return. Clodagh further agrees that she will not discuss with her son Michael Anchorage that he is the child's father and will maintain that William's real mother had passed away in childbirth. The sum of one hundred thousand pounds has been provided in order that suitable alternative accommodation can be found but must be outside of Trellinick and the surrounding area, and for the duration of the child's care.

Signed: *Clodagh Anchorage*

Date: *22nd April 1972*

Marjorie May Hepburn agrees that all ties with the infant William Michael Anchorage will cease and that no attempt to contact either Clodagh Anchorage or William Michael Anchorage will ever be made. I freely relinquish all claims to the child and any decisions relating to his upbringing or care. I will from this day forward play no role in his life.

Only the Lonely

On the reverse, handwritten in fading ink was a message Clodagh had clearly added:

To the finder of this agreement,

I am writing this on the eve of baby William's first Christmas.

I will willingly raise William as my own. He is my grandson, and his welfare will always be my priority. However, it is my belief that his mother Marjorie Hepburn did not willingly surrender her baby as this agreement suggests. Circumstance and threats from her somewhat tyrannical mother have meant that Marjorie was left with no choice. For my part, I agreed to sign this document to avoid Violet involving the authorities and placing William with a family outside of his own. This was a threat I had no doubt she would carry through.

If you feel the timing is right for all parties or in the event of my death, please let Marjorie know where her son has been raised and by whom. You must also inform my son Michael that William is his son and not as he has always believed, his adopted brother.

Clodagh Anchorage

24th December 1972

I folded the letter back up and placed it back in the envelope. The circle of lies and deceit was now complete, and I was at the centre of it. I sat motionless on the bed, stunned. My mind was jolted back into the room when I heard Michael shouting for me to help him move a chest to the van. It was then that I realised for the first time that the voice shouting to me did in fact belong to my dad and not my brother. I said nothing about the letter to Michael at the time. I was just so rocked by it all. My mind was reeling. Michael noticed that I was clearly distracted, however, and teased me about whether it was doing a bit of real physical work that had made me go quiet. I forced a smile back at him and replied he was just an accountant; real work was conducted by architects and builders.

Days passed and having discussed it all with Sofia, I decided that I would try to find my mother.

I turned again to the agreement relating to my adoption. Was this even a legally binding contract? Surely this was not how agreements to raise children were designed and implemented? It seemed so harsh and almost confrontational. What was hard to accept was that this appeared to indicate that my mother had indeed given me away and that hurt deeply. It was only Clodagh's guess that she hadn't.

I contacted a solicitor who reviewed the agreement. He confirmed that it was clearly unprofessionally constructed with no legal basis and was written by one of the parties who was not well-versed in law. Not unusual for the back then.

I had been conducting some research with the advice of my solicitor and over dinner, I told Sofia what I had uncovered. In spite of her expressing her real and genuine concerns for me, I insisted that I still wanted to see what I could find out about Trellinick and who Marjorie Hepburn was.

I found Trellinick on the map and the following weekend on a brisk April morning Sofia and I drove out to take a look.

We both loved the village immediately. We parked the car at the top of the village and walked down the quaint high street with its boxed flowers, Cornish flag flying proudly from the village green, and a small, very well-stocked store and coffee shop. We went inside and ordered coffees to drink outside. When the waitress brought the coffee out to us, it was clear that she was pleased to have customers on an otherwise inclement day; clearly customers had been few and far between.

She asked whether we were holidaymakers, and I replied we were not, that we were just driving through and stopped because the village looked so lovely. She seemed to beam with pride at our enthusiasm for the village and explained that she and her husband Simon owned and managed the shop and café. She went on to explain that they also owned the small mobile home park just down the lane behind their store. Beachcombers, Trellinick's best kept secret.

She was incredibly friendly and took a great interest in the upcoming arrival of our baby and where in Bath we lived. She then introduced herself as Milly. Sparing no detail, she explained to us how her husband Simon had not wanted to farm the land which they had inherited from her parents, so they had developed a small and beautiful mobile home park on the land.

I asked if the mobile home park was actually on the beach and she explained that it overlooked the bay, but the beach could be accessed through a gate at the back and down a short treelined lane to the bay itself.

"One of the residents, Marjorie, goes down to the beach every single morning, come rain, wind, or shine. She takes herself off down there and has her cup of tea on the bench at the dunes around seven thirty every morning. Lost in thought no doubt, but savouring the beauty of the bay too.

You should go and have a look. There's a public footpath that runs along the outside of the park and joins the little lane at the bottom. It's not a private beach but I think sometimes we feel it is. There's really only us who know about it. This bay is only really used by us and the Beachcomber residents."

Again, my heart skipped a beat but this time at the mention of my mother's name. Surely for such a small park there couldn't be more than one Marjorie on the site. I wanted to make sure.

"Ah, Marjorie, that's a lovely name. You don't hear that often these days, do you?"

"Yes, that's true. Our Marjorie Hepburn is one in a million, that's for sure. Like us, born and raised here in Trellinick. She's lived at Beachcombers since it opened and loves it. She never married but that's for another day. I'd need more than a cappuccino to explain that heart-breaking story to you. Anyway, I best get on. Simon always tells me off for chatting for too long"

Sofia and I walked down the lane and found the bay with

the solitary bench overlooking the sea. Sofia saw the tears pooling in my eyes and held onto my arms. "I'm sorry, Will. That was so hard."

"Sofia, what the heck went on here. Why has mother, my real mother, been left alone all these years. I can't bear it. It's just too sad. It's so very sad."

We sat on what was Marjorie's bench looking out across the bay. We saw the tiny boats rise and fall behind the waves. We saw the gulls swoop and dive for stolen catch, and we were silent. My eyes again filled with tears as I thought about her sitting there on her own every morning drinking her tea. That money Clodagh had given to us wasn't mine, it was Marjorie's. I felt I had to return it to her and thought about what Milly had just told me about Marjorie's routine.

A week later I returned to Trellinick. This time laden with a black Nike holdall and two large rocks I'd found on the beach. I clambered onto the dunes, battling strengthening winds, and placed the bag next to the lone bench at the top of the dunes hidden by marron grass. Marjorie's bench. My mothers bench. I then hunkered down and waited. At just after eight o'clock, the lady arrived and sat on her bench. The scene was exactly how I pictured it. Though it was hard to see her fully against the gale blowing the hood of her raincoat back and forth and the fringe of her hair blowing frantically against her knitted hat, this was clearly the lady Milly had described partaking of her daily routine. This was clearly my mother.

I lay in the dunes and watched her pour her tea and eat what looked like a teacake. I had to resist the urge to run through the dunes and hug her. In spite of my efforts and promise to Sofia I wouldn't get upset, I couldn't stop the tears from welling in my eyes. That innocent woman sipping tea - unaware of the truth of her story, of our story. I wanted to bide my time. I had no real way of knowing how she felt about me. I only had Clodagh's word on the back of the contract that my mother had been forced to surrender me. I'd waited my entire life to meet her – I could wait a little longer.

I saw her notice the bag. She'd leaned forward and surveyed it but from her bench. Rather than walk over to it however, she finished her tea and gathered up what looked like a radio and cushion and left the beach. I couldn't believe it. I sunk my forehead into the sand against the driving wind. Once I was sure she had left, I ran across the dunes, picked the bag up and ran back to my car. I spoke with Sofia, and we decided to give it one more try the following day. If she doesn't look inside the bag the following day, we'd have another think.

This was starting to feel like a crazy plan, but I was just determined to return the money to her, then in time, explain its origins to her. That money was hers. It was her inheritance. I had written her name on the tag on the side of the bag so she would at least know that she was the intended recipient *'To Marjorie from a secret benefactor.'*

When I reflected on this plan, I realised how crazy it was. Even if she finally collected the bag, it would probably rock her world completely. I risked her handing it in to the Police for starters. If that happened, I was confident once we did finally meet, we could legitimately reclaim it from them - I'd be able to show them the paper trail. What I really hoped was that she'd take the money and have some fun with it. I had no idea what my mother considered fun of course, but I hoped the money would help her experience something joyful.

With the bag safely back in my car I made the short drive to Padstow, found a hotel and bunkered down for the evening. The procedure would be repeated in the morning.

I returned to the beach at seven in the morning. I struggled across the dune and replaced the bag where it had been the previous morning. The wind was still swirling across the dunes, forcing the fine sand to swirl and skim across the mounds and settle amongst the brittle grasses.

At eight O'clock she arrived. Wrapped up in a scarf and hat, she sat on her bench with her cushion, flask and tiny radio. Again, she looked across at the bag. This time, curiosity got the better of her, she walked over and opened it. I had to put my hand over my mouth to muffle my laughter at her reaction to what the bag contained. After a further period of surveillance, she left the beach with the bag and my plans for now at least, were completed. How strange to watch the mother I had never known sipping tea just feet away from me.

I watched her carry the bag away, I stayed motionless hidden on the beach for a further hour, just taking in the dramatic scenes being thrown up by the storm. This place really was magical. As I stood up to leave, I hoped that the note I had attached to the bag wouldn't confuse or worry her too much and that she would appreciate that this selfless gesture was a gift to her from an 'secret benefactor'. I also hoped the gale hadn't liberated it as she wrestled to pick the bag up from it hidden position in the grasses.

On reflection, I should probably have put the note inside the bag, but I feared she may not realise the bag was for her and simply leave it there. I knew in time I would be able to explain it all to her. I had waited fifty years to know my mother, but for Clodagh's sake and out of my unfailing love and loyalty towards her, I could, for now at least, wait a little longer.

CHAPTER FORTY-FIVE
Marjorie

We spent the rest of the morning and into the afternoon, reunited with our darling friend Albert. Though Hetty had offered the floor to me, it was she who had us both laughing uncontrollably as she recounted the many tales and experiences afforded us from just three days away from the solemnity of Beachcombers. She is just the best storyteller, though I kept my wits about me ready to jump in in case she mentioned our trip to 'Ann Summers'. Poor Albert would have been horrified.

Thankfully she was, on this occasion at least, subtle enough to leave that detail out. As the afternoon drifted towards evening, I felt tired so at five o'clock, I risked walking across the park in my new dressing gown and slippers and returned home for a power nap. (Hetty called it a nanna nap and now that I knew I was a nanna, I was happy enough to accept that).

I left Hetty with Albert, just as she'd helped herself to a bottle of a 'chilled white' from Albert's fridge. I could sense the pair of them were up for an evening giddy with funny stories and a few cheeky glasses of wine so chose to make my exit before I felt obliged to join them. I wasn't being miserable; I was just weary and overwhelmed from the last few days. I think they both understood I had a great deal to process.

When I got home, I went through to my turned down bed. I had prepared it in a fashion I had become accustomed to from my new favourite hotel. That makes it sound like I had a previous favourite hotel. In fact, I don't, but nevertheless, The Savoy is now definitely number one.

Only the Lonely

I may not have had a little chocolate for my pillow, but I was happy enough to fill that gap with my biscuits. After I showered, I popped on my fresh pyjamas and walked through to my living room. I modelled my new Savoy dressing gown to no-one but myself in the mirror. I sat in my favourite chair listening to the silence. I sipped my tea, nibbled my biscuit and for the first time I felt an excitement for the future I had never previously experienced. I was still mindful that as I sat sipping my tea, my home was harbouring a considerable amount of elicit cash. For now, I wasn't going to allow that to spoil this moment. The five thousand pounds hidden in my linen cupboard could wait.

I took my phone from my handbag and there were two messages. The first was a photograph from Hetty. She was wearing Albert's dressing gown and he hers - they had clearly enjoyed the first bottle of wine, so goodness knew what time she'd get to bed. The second message was from Harry. I dug out my reading glasses, and with my fire crackling quietly as it warmed the room and pressed on the envelope to open his message.

Hi Marjorie,
Hope you got home safely. I just wanted to let you know that I have had a message from Clodagh. William and Michael have now been informed of their true relationship to you and to each other. She feels sure they will be in touch with you. Are you fine with me giving them your mobile phone number?
I hope you're doing okay Marjorie, I know this has been an enormous shock to you.
Best. Harry.

I went through to the kitchen and poured myself a little glass of port. I looked at the roses Albert had given me at the station. He knew I loved cream roses, and these were particularly beautiful. I sat looking at them and realised I was crying. I wasn't altogether sure why. I think it was a mixture of joy at the fact that I might once again hold William mixed with the real sadness that it had ever got to this point; a reunion with the son I always loved but who I was prevented from loving.

I wiped away my tears and told myself that I was being silly but for all the internalising and berating of myself for being so emotional, the tears kept coming. I think I was drained with it all. Not just the last few days, weeks or even months, but with a lifetime of longing. I don't really know how to describe the feeling or explain how it attacked me in waves. William's absence from my life had always overshadowed any joy or achievements my life had blessed me with. I hadn't even had a photograph of him. Not a physical one, at least.

When he was first taken, I would often lie in my bed and picture his little face so that I wouldn't forget him. I could replay in my mind the little noises he made as I fed him and the tiny movements of his fingers as I cradled him. But, of course, time is a thief, and I reached a point where I could no longer be specific about how my baby had looked. Being with Hetty's babies, though a constant joy, also confused my mind, replacing William's memory.

I finished my port, finally dried my tears, and sat quietly, listening to the crackling of the fire and the whistling of the wind around my beautiful home. I looked for spaces on my walls and surfaces where I could put pictures of my son, grandson and soon my second grandchild.

I assessed as only I could, where I might store toys, should they come to visit. When I felt ready, I got up and went through to the kitchen and got my little breakfast bag out ready for the morning. My china cup was ready along with the tin foil for my teacake. I could feel the warm glow to my cheeks that the port had generated and decided I would have another rather than tea and biscuits and take it to my turned down bed. Another day as a mother and grandmother complete.

CHAPTER FORTY-SIX
Hetty

I got home from Albert's and poured a large glass of iced water. What had just happened? How on earth could that be? I felt very weary, but my head was alive from it all. I'd loved seeing Albert's joy at us being back again - it almost made going away in the first place so worthwhile. Then for him to drop Charlie's name into the conversation and it uncover such an unbelievable coincidence was just too much. I'd gathered so much strength and peace in knowing Edwin was not part of what I had here, yet now I know he has a heart-breaking link to Albert's story.

I quickly showered and as I walked around my bedroom, Marjorie popped into my mind. I smiled at the thought she had no doubt turned her bed down as soon as she got home tonight. Inevitably that would become her new routine now she knew it was what the upper classes did. I wondered what she had done with 'Alan Titchmarsh'. I imagined he was well hidden as I knew was the remainder of the cash.

I looked at my own non-turned-down bed and smiled to myself. No sign of a chocolate or my slippers neatly side by side waiting for me. I hung my amazing new dressing gown up behind my bedroom door, discarding my older, well-worn one to go into recycling. My mobile phone lit up and there was a message from Brodie. I decided not to reply, but to call him. I had the warm blanket of pinot spurring me on, so I dialled his number. Two hours later, we ended the call. What was happening to me. I hadn't intended to allow anybody into my life again, but Brodie seemed to have ignited something. It was imperceptibly small, but there.

He had explained that he was coming to Plymouth for a few days to look at property and would love to see me again. It was early days, of course, but it was the first time in so long that a man had made me feel special. We hadn't even kissed so I knew I was being ridiculous and forward, but still, I couldn't help but feel a little excited.

As soon as I climbed into bed, I felt wide awake again. Thoughts were dancing around my head, jumping from memory to memory. I told myself to sleep but it was as if my mind had unfinished business that it needed me to tend to first. Not prepared to fight with myself any longer, I sat up and went through the photographs on my phone. It was such a memorable trip. I had never actually experienced anything like it before and doubted I would again.

Then my thoughts turned back to my conversation with Albert. Comparing his situation with Kathleen to my own with Edwin, it made the history of their situation even more tragic to me. If I thought the love was lost between them or that Kathleen had found someone new then that would be different. The truth was clear; he still loved her. Tonight was the first time ever that Albert had discussed his feelings for Kathleen or indeed become tearful and I have known him for ten years.

He was not like Marjorie and I; we shared everything. We knew everything about each other. Albert was more of a closed book. I was no psychologist, but what was clear from tonight was that he just feared rejection. I think he suffered so much pain back then, not surprisingly, he let his emotions drive his decision-making and that is often a confusing thing to do. Maybe while Marjorie and I had been away he'd had time to reflect on loneliness. For some reason his lingering feelings for Kathleen had resurfaced. I couldn't imagine that us uncovering such a weird connection tonight would have helped either. I still couldn't believe it.

What Kathleen did was wrong but turning love on and off was so hard. In my case, it was a slow bleeding to death over many years. For Albert social norms dictated that, when your marriage vows had been so affronted, you must stop loving that person from that point forward. But human emotions don't work like that. We're not taps to be turned on and off. We are complex and love hurts.

The rights and wrongs of what Kathleen did, her true motivation for sleeping with this Charlie guy, would only ever truly be known, or understood by her. I just prayed that these two people who were clearly put on this earth to love each other, could finally find a way to forgive and rebuild what they had.

I clambered back out of bed and walked through to my living room. I remembered that many years ago, Marjorie had thought it would be a jolly good idea if we all shared our emergency contact details with one another. I scrambled through my 'everything drawer' (don't judge me, everyone has one - well, except Marjorie, she has an everything-neatly-filed drawer). At the back I found the piece of paper. There it was. Albert had provided both Emily and Kathleen's details. While the distress of seeing Albert's tearful admission was still clear in my mind, I would call her in the morning.

I would not however mention Edwin and the accident. That was something Albert could tell her if, and when, he felt it right to do so. I wasn't even sure how that conversation would go, '*hi Kathleen we don't know each other but my husband killed your lover.*' No, that was definitely a decision and conversation Albert should have with her when he felt ready.

Now wide awake, I made a cup tea and lay on the sofa, propped up with cushions, cosy in my new dressing gown with a fluffy blanket over my toes. I then put on an episode of my absolute favourite show, Call the Midwife, from my Sky planner and instantly fell asleep.

When I woke it was to the sound of the gulls screeching and the wind rattling against my window that stirred me. It was light but it still took me a few seconds to orientate myself back in my own home and not in the luxury I had become accustomed to at The Savoy. I remembered instantly that I had resolved to make contact with Kathleen this morning but remained unsure of how I would broach the subject of reuniting Albert with her. I honestly believe in life you should strike while the iron's hot.

I was determined not to let Albert's admission last night disappear into the ether with Kathleen never having heard how he now felt about her. I was probably in danger of poking my nose in, or interfering but what was there to lose here? If Kathleen knocked me back, so be it, I'd say nothing to Albert, and we'd carry on. 'He who dares wins', hey Albert. I'd risk being shouted at by your feisty Celtic sweetheart.

I dressed and made a pot of tea and walked back into my living room. It was a calmer day and although Marjorie would no doubt be back from her morning walk by now, I didn't need to wonder about the logic of sitting on the beach on mornings like this – it was glorious. It was now 9.30 and I felt sure most people would be awake, so it was not an impolite time to call. My tummy was in complete turmoil as I picked up the piece of paper and typed her number into my phone.

It rang immediately and after all but three rings she answered. 'Hello, Kathleen speaking.'

"Oh hi, Kathleen, look we don't actually know each other, but my name is Hetty. I live next door to Albert. He's fine, don't worry, I just wanted to talk to you about a conversation I had with Albert last night. He doesn't know I am ringing you. Look, is this a good time to talk?"

"Yeah sure, Hetty, hi, Emily has mentioned you, and Marjorie. Is everything okay?"

"Honestly, everything is fine. Look, Kathleen, I'm just going to come out with it. I know what happened in the past, you know, between you and Albert, and how you both struggled to sort things out. I'm not judging at all; I just want you to know that I understand the history between you. Well, last night he and I were chatting over a bottle of wine, and he told me that he still loves you, Kathleen. He's said it in the past, don't get me wrong, but this time it was different. This time it was emotional, deep. He doesn't know how to reach out to you now as it's been so long. I just wanted you to know that's all, what you do with this is up to you. He's terrified of rejection; I could see it in him. I'm not telling you this to make you feel guilty, Kathleen, or to interfere, but I just thought if you felt the same way, what a bloody shame that you two can't find a way to sort things out - whatever that means."

There was silence on the other end of the line, and I wondered if I had lost connection, "Hello, Kathleen?"

"Yes, Hetty, I'm here, don't worry. I'm just a bit shocked. Why did he say that, where has that come from?"

"I just asked him about how he had come to Cornwall, and he opened up, saying being close to you back then was a constant battle between love and hurt and he couldn't carry on that way. He thought if he moved away, a long way away, it would give you both time and space to heal. It clearly hasn't worked though, love is love, Kathleen. Your man still loves you."

"I don't quite know what to say, Hetty. I'm a bit blown away with it all. I won't discuss what happened between us with you, I'm sure you understand. It's so painful and private. I honestly believed he had found a way to live without me and had moved on."

"Well, that's the skill of a master actor, Kathleen, isn't it? He has done both of those things. He has moved on and he has learnt to live without you, but that doesn't mean he's happy about it. He is clearly an actor in a play he has no desire to be in. His lines are well rehearsed and beautifully delivered, but I think we both know now, his time in this play is over. I think he's tired Kathleen. He's worked on his acting for long enough, his mask slipped last night, and the truth was revealed.

You have my number now Kathleen, call me whenever you like. If I'm with him, I'll make my excuses and leave. If your heart is telling you the same as Albert's though Kathleen, then maybe you know what you have to do. Please feel you can stay in touch with me."

"Thank you Hetty. Thank you so very much. I can't imagine calling me was easy, so thank you for taking the trouble. I will of course stay in touch with you. I need to take stock first and of course I will talk with Emily. Or maybe I won't. Oh gosh, I'm just so confused. You're right, I just need to take stock. Thank you again, Hetty, I will be in touch, but I just need to think carefully, for Albert's and Emily's sake. I will call you again and we'll

talk. My mind is everywhere.
Oh my goodness, Albie.
Thank you, Hetty."

CHAPTER FORTY-SEVEN
Marjorie

I rose at seven to be greeted by the familiar sound of the sea lapping against the rocks of Trellinick Bay. The winds of the previous night had subsided, and the morning sky was now a rich royal blue with candyfloss clouds moving slowly across its surface. I sat in my living room and drank my lemon tea, absentmindedly watching the distant waves and the gathering gulls as they swooped and dived over my home and headed back out across the bay. I felt whole again. For the first time, possibly ever in my life, I even felt optimistic.

I showered and dressed, picked up my breakfast bag and made my way to the dunes and my bench. Unlike the day when I had found the money, today was not going to be stormy. The sun had barely risen over the distant cliffs, which against the darkness seemed to be disappearing into the sea. I sat on my bench, and watched, transfixed by the white tops of turquoise blue waves just visible against the sky whilst the darkened silhouettes of the dancing grasses and golden dunes were starting to come into focus. It was a warm breeze that brushed against my face, I turned slightly to feel its warmth against my skin. Much as I had enjoyed my time in London, these were the sights and sounds that were much more comforting and familiar than those I had encountered in London.

I took out my toasted teacake and poured myself a cup of tea. I watched the swirl of steam give itself up to the breeze. I took comfort in noting that nothing had changed. The trawlers still swayed and curled against the swell. The tiny particles of sand were still being pushed and pulled across the flattened beach by the gentle winds, and the smell and spray of sea air still clung to my hair as my tiny teacup still warmed my hands. As I sipped my tea I thought again, nothing has changed. But in truth, I knew, everything had changed.

I hadn't heard the footsteps.

I hadn't heard the rustle of jackets, the crunching of pebbles nor the breathing of the two people standing behind my bench.

Until the first one spoke.

CHAPTER FORTY-EIGHT
Albert

My conversation with Hetty had moved me. For the first time since my separation, I had spoken the words out loud; I still loved Kathleen. As much now as I ever did. What a proud old fool I had been by isolating myself from her all these years.

Hetty had reignited something in me. Had homed in on something I'd long put to the back of my mind. Perhaps all the turmoil caused by Marjorie's beach discovery, her potential reunion with William and the possible new love interest of Hetty and this Brodie chap had unsettled or refocused me.

With my friend's absence in London and three days spent with Emily, I'd had a chance to think. To really think. Much as I missed my friends, the deeper pain was actually staring me in the face. I missed my family. I missed what we had and what we were. I only ever had fifty percent with me when I shared time with Emily. The other half was somewhere distant. Isolated from me. At my behest

I knew Hetty was right. Life was too short. The strange and unsettling connection of Hetty to Charlie McBride's tragic passing was surely testament to that. Her husband's sad demise into alcoholism and the terrible accident leading to Charlie's death affected so many lives. Perhaps it was time for me to see past how Kathleen hurt me. She'd created a life in Emily and that made me the happiest man alive. That joy never wavered. I think it was time for me to move beyond resentment. To focus on the future with Kathleen.

Only the Lonely

Was that even possible?

CHAPTER FORTY-NINE
Kathleen

I'd woken with the intention of producing revision notes for students studying Law at Kingston University. The second-year module on Forensic Criminology had given rise to many sleepless nights for the students I tutored. I'd retired from my own law firm and now enjoyed the interactions I had with the next generation of solicitors. I gave my time freely as they were a great source of fun to me and I'm sure my lack of knowledge of YouTube and IT generally was to them. It was a symbiotic relationship that worked for all involved.

I had just sat at my laptop with a freshly brewed coffee when my mobile phone rang. I did not recognise the number and despite my usual practice of ignoring unfamiliar numbers, I chose to answer.

Hetty.

I sat nursing my coffee. I don't believe I took a single breath as she spoke. I listened as her words fell into the solemnity of my study. Her voice was steady but passionate. It was clear she found the conversation as emotional to say as it was for me to hear.

I'd heard so much about Hetty from Emily and knew how much she meant to Albert. It must mean something if he'd confided his inner most feelings to her. Albert had always been a reserved man, not given to sharing or expressing his feelings.

I'd experienced at a very great cost to my life that knowledge can be a dangerous ally. I had kept from Albert a terrible secret and it had cost me my marriage. I had the knowledge that Emily may not have been his child but did nothing with it. I wasn't going to do that a second time to him.

I ended the call with Hetty. Closed the laptop and dialled his number. Hetty had suggested I wait and take stock. But I'd spent years doing that. I wanted to hear Alberts voice. I wanted to him say he wanted 'us' again.

CHAPTER FIFTY
Marjorie

I sat still on my bench; hands wrapped tightly around my cup. The sea stretched before me as it pulled away, whispering secrets I had spent a lifetime trying to hear. A silver lake across the sand I had always known.

"Mum."

My heart lurched, thrown out of rhythm. Time, for a moment, stood still. It couldn't be him.

I stood slowly not daring to turn around. My legs trembled but held. I paused and tried to gather myself as I turned and there he was. William. My son.

Beside him stood the unmistakable figure of Michael, his father.

My hands flew to my mouth. I tried to remember how to breathe. My head spun. It was them. My son, and his father.

For so many years I had thought William was my only loss. But as I looked at the two men standing before me, I realised that Michael had been a loss too. He had been my only love and seeing him again was a pain I did not recognise, had not prepared for.

William was taller than Michael. Broad-shouldered. A quiet intensity behind his deep brown eyes. And something else. A fear I recognised instantly, because I had carried it too.

He stared at me as though trying to work out who I was, not the name, not the story, but the meaning of me to him.

"I" he began, then faltered. "I don't know what to say,

Mum."

"You don't have to say anything, my love," I said, my voice breaking. "You're here. You're both here."

He looked down at his hands. "I'm so sorry mum, for all the lying and deception. For the pain it has obviously caused you. Clodagh, my grandmother told me Michael was my brother. That I was her second baby, adopted because you'd died delivering me."

I felt my breath catch, but I didn't look away.

"You were my first, William. There was never another. Michael is not your older brother. He's your father. I suspect you already know that."

His face crumpled. Tears welled. "Why, Mum? Why did all this happen to us?"

I walked to him. My fingers trembled as they reached for his face.

"Because I was young. Because I was alone. And because people made choices for me they had no right to make."

Then I fell into his opened arms. I felt the tears begin, and once they came, they would not stop.

Fifty years of missed birthdays and Christmases. Of silence. My tears carried both the ache of what was stolen and the wonder of what had somehow returned. I held him as if he might be taken from me again. Pain and joy, all at once.

In that moment I saw again the dreadful morning Violet had dragged him from my arms whilst he slept. His hand slipping from the blanket. The soft exhale as he was carried away, from my room, from my life.

Michael stepped forward, quietly.

"I am so sorry, Marjorie. For the part I played in this. I was as deceived as you. I promise you. I had no idea William was my son – our son. I am selfishly grateful I helped raise him, but for everything you missed, and for all the reasons why, I am destroyed." His voice was low and broken.

I composed myself, reached for his hand. I could see the pain he was feeling. I'd seen it once before. The night he told me he was leaving Trellinick.

"We were all lied to Michael. All of us deceived. What a web. I was lied to with selfish, evil intent. To Violet, William was an obstacle. An inconvenience she couldn't live with. In Clodagh's case, I believe she thought she was doing the right thing. I bear her no ill will.

For all these years, I believed you had no idea you had a child. That we had a child. There you were, just a boy, helping to raise a child you didn't know was yours. William grew up believing you were his brother. I believed he'd been adopted by a family in Norfolk. All of it lies. He lived so close to me, yet so far."

I turned back to William. I breathed him in. His scent, his softness, his presence.

"I used to wonder who held you. I wondered if they sang to you at night, as I had when I was pregnant, and for the one magical week I had you in my arms. I never stopped loving you."

He broke in, his voice raw.

"I don't know how to hold all of this. I feel like I'm made of someone else's mistakes."

"No," I said, turning to him fully. "You were made from love. I loved you every day of your life William. Even when I didn't know where you were. Even when the world tried to make me forget. That kind of love doesn't vanish. It waits.

"Your father and I made you out of love. You are not a mistake. You are the most beautiful part of us."

He stepped forward slowly, as if the ground might vanish beneath his feet.

I held him tightly, my cheek pressed to his shoulder, breathing in the man he had become and the boy I never got to raise.

"I found you," he whispered. "I found you again. I'm just so sorry it took so long."

Behind us, Michael turned away, shoulders shaking. But I reached out for him, wordlessly. Forgiveness offered not in speech, but in the simple outstretching of my fingers.

He took my hand.

The three of us stood on the sand, the wind rushing past,

the sea rising and falling. The past too heavy to carry alone any longer. But somehow, between us, we held it.

We sat holding each other until peace calmed us. Three souls reunited on a bench on a beach that held so many stories.

"But how did you find me? How did you know I would be here?"

"The lady who runs the shop and café, I think she's called Milly. I came here a few months ago. She told me all about you."

"What? A few months ago."

I looked from William to Michael then back to William again. "What do you mean a few months ago? I only just found out about where you were days ago from a private investigator I hired to find you. How can you have known about me for months? I don't understand."

"Clodagh, I mean my grandmother, did tell us her story last week. But I'd already found you myself. This is quite a tale mum. Do you want to hear it here, or back at you house?"

I leant back against the security of the bench. I looked at both my boys and smiled, my tears drained and contained once more. The emotion and shock at seeing and holding my boys had turned to joy. A joy I had previously only dared to dream of. How was any of this happening. William had found me and only months before I had found him. Our paths destined to cross again.

"Let's walk back. There's two people I'd like you both to meet. Michael you won't be surprised who one of them is."

"Don't tell me - Hetty." My smile confirmed he was correct. "I can't believe you're still friends after all these years. William make sure you stay by me - if she hasn't changed, a handsome man like you isn't safe around her."

"Well yes. Your father is right there William. Mind you, she may be taken on that front so you might be safe son."

"Son. I just called you son. You have no idea how I've longed to say that simple word." William smiled back at me, "It's incredible to hear you say it mum."

With arms linked we walked back to my home. They sat in my living room, seemingly surveying it all as I texted my two companions.

It's happened again. An incredible discovery on the beach. Not a bag filled with money this time. Not a shell with the face of Jesus either Hetty. Come immediately. Mx

---

CHAPTER FIFTY-ONE
Hetty

I had intended to spend the day doing the mundane things that always need attention after time away. Washing, cleaning, shopping. But two people had put pay to that idea.

The first was Brodie.

His property search in Plymouth had proven fruitless, so he was going to stay down there and view more places later in the week. That meant he would not be far from Trellinick. So, the inevitable happened. I invited him to my house for lunch.

I was shocked by how forward I was being, but in that moment I decided life was too short not to grab happiness when it presents itself. If it amounted to nothing, fair enough. At least I'd dipped my toe in.

Brodie had reignited something in me, for the first time in years, I felt attractive again. Not just a mother and grandmother. Perhaps I could be a partner again. So far, he had been the perfect gentleman. He assured me that his little manoeuvre at the bar in London, sending drinks over to Marjorie and me, was the first time he had ever done anything like that.

The cynic in me doubted it, but the romantic in me was happy to believe him.

I was about to go and tell Albert the latest development when the second person to change my plans for the day sent a message to our group chat.

Marjorie.

She had clearly been out roaming on the beach again,

and her text made it clear she had found something else. Not money this time, but something that required our attention nonetheless.

I arrived at Albert's to find him sitting at the dining table, phone in hand. He had clearly just read Marjorie's message too, but there was a look on his face I could not read.

"You okay, Albie? What's up? Surely that's not Lady M's text that's got you looking like that?"

"No. I've been chatting with Kathleen. I saw Marjorie's message. I'll come now. But Hetty, Kathleen just called me. She wants to come over at the weekend, without Emily. She wants us to go out for dinner. To talk."

"Oh gosh, Albert. How do you feel? I wonder what made her decide to call now. Remember what you told me - you still love her. Grab it, Albert. Don't let this chance pass you by. Yes she did a terrible thing. But try and understand why. I'm still reeling from what we realised last night about Charlie McBride. Surely his tragic story is proof, life is too short."

"I don't know how to feel. I'm shocked. I mean, I'm thrilled too. But mostly shocked. She said Morag reached out to her a few months ago, said she missed seeing us. I don't know if that rattled Kathleen or made her nostalgic. Whatever the reason, I said yes. Kathleen is coming here."

"There must be something in the water, Albie. I'm meeting Brodie for lunch here this week too. He's in Plymouth, so he's coming across and I'm making dinner. If my cooking doesn't test the depths of his intentions, nothing will."

Albert laughed but scolded me for being so critical of my cooking. I knew I was being modest. I made a very good goulash and was accomplished with anything pasta themed.

We shared a quick hug and decided to keep our romantic developments from Marjorie for now. Her latest beach discovery needed to be the topic of conversation.

CHAPTER FIFTY-TWO
Marjorie

I walked through to my living room and smiled at my two guests. I still couldn't quite believe who was sat in my house. Little did they know they were sat amongst forty thousand pounds of hidden, mysteriously acquired cash, the other forty hidden at Hetty's. "Tea, coffee or something stronger?"

They were both quick to opt for the something stronger option, confirming they had booked rooms at the hotel so wouldn't be driving home later. I returned with five glasses and two bottles of chilled wine. I placed them on the coffee table as I saw Hetty and Albert link arms and make their way to my home.

Hetty entered first and without drawing breath she turned to Michael. "Oh, my goodness Michael Anchorage. You haven't changed a bit. She ran and put her arms around him. Don't tell me this is William? No way! Are you William?" She looked to me and seeing my smile she ran to him. "Oh my god William, you have no idea. Your mother has missed you her entire life. I can't believe you're finally here. You are the double of your father. Your eyes, my goodness they are like Galaxy Minstrels. How? What? What's happening here. How have you two got here. Marjorie explain. What's going on? I take it William and Michael are the latest beach discoveries"

Albert then spoke, "Well this is a clearly long overdue reunion. I'm delighted to meet you both. I'm Albert Hargraves, your mothers neighbour and friend. William and Michael, how very lovely to meet you both."

I opened the wine and filled the five glasses.

"Bloody hell. I can't get my head around this. I thought you were going to take stock for a while Marjorie. How has this happened." Hetty was looking from me to William and Michael then back to me.

I handed the wine around then went and sat next to William who took hold of my hand. "I'm as in the dark as you are Hetty. William, we're all together now, please I'm desperate to know, how did you find me?"

Hetty stood, her hand running through her hair. "Wait, what? William found you?"

"Yes, William and Michael found me. Come on William, we're all ears."

He then explained to a silent room how he had found the contract his grandmother had signed, ordered to do so by Violet. He handed it to me, but I didn't open it. I hung onto his every word, desperate to soak up the sound of his voice and the emotion of his story. For the first time I was hearing life from his perspective. I wiped my tears away and handed tissues to Hetty who was somewhat overcome with it all.

The bigger shock was to come as he explained how he had returned the inheritance. He felt uncomfortable keeping the money Violet had given his grandmother for his care. It was my inheritance, and he wanted to return it to me. Nervous about actually confronting me with it all, he hatched a plan to return the money back to where he felt it belonged. In my hands.

He'd placed it on my beach, by my bench in a NIKE bag weighted down by two rocks.

Hetty couldn't hold her silence any longer.

"What the actual fuck! That money was left by you William. Are you kidding me. Do you have any idea what we've been through since your mother found that bag. It's been like living with an overly paranoid bank robber. Albert even rang a solicitor friend about it - to check we weren't all going to jail for keeping it."

Whilst William attempted to apologise for causing the upset, we couldn't help but laugh at the irony of it all. The money was legitimately left for me to find. The note William had left for me had obviously been blown off in the wind. I then used fifteen thousand pounds of the money to find him, when he'd already found me. I'd never seen Albert quite so amused or animated by anything before and I loved it.

Hetty then continued through her laughter.

"William don't open that pot on the fireplace, there's two thousand pounds in there. Oh, and if you use the bathroom, don't unravel the towel pyramid at the back of the bath, that contains five thousand pounds."

I explained that I had used part of the money to employ the services of a private investigator. He had found and made contact with Clodagh who had written a letter explaining the story of William's life. The remainder of the money had been hidden in my house and Hetty's house. I assured William that the money would now be deposited in the bank in order that I could finally return to sleeping safely in my bed.

Once the dust had somewhat settled on the tales that had filled the room, William took out his phone and showed us all photographs of Sofia and Oscar. I encouraged Michael to shows us photographs of his children Evie and Joey. I could tell he was being reticent, but they were his family, and I wanted from the outset for him to know that I understood his life had continued away from Trellinick. Joey looked very much like William, I stopped short of asking if Evie was like her mother, there had been enough tears shed.

I quietly relished being present in William's life for the arrival of their new baby. I wondered if the memory of holding him as a baby however fleetingly, would be reignited.

I went through to the kitchen to get more wine as William followed me. He asked that we have some time alone. I readily agreed. We grabbed coats and walked back down to the beach leaving a very animated living room of chatter and wine glass clinking.

We sat on my bench as late morning drew the tide back in and a slight chill on the breeze.

"Can you believe all of this mum? No sorry that's wrong. Can you believe any of this mum?"

"No William I can't. I really can't. If this wasn't

happening to me, if this was a novel, I'd say it's way too farfetched. A stolen baby, a bag of money, a private detective, a reunion and a bench on a beach. No son, I really can't believe it."

I put my head on his shoulder and felt his breathing. Slow and rhythmic. A sound I had longed to hear and feel for fifty years.

"Mum how would you feel if Sofia, Oscar and I all moved here?"

I sat up. "What? What do you mean William? You want to move to Trellinick, to Beachcombers?"

"Well not Beachcombers exactly. Dad, Sofia and I have been talking to Milly and Simon. See that broken greenhouse across there, and the land it's sat on? Well, that whole plot is available and they would be delighted for me to build on that land. I'm a local you see mum, born in Trellinick I was."

"William I don't know what to say. I'd be delighted. Is Sofia fine about moving. I mean it's a lot to ask of her."

"Yes, she's just as excited as I am. Oscar will love it down here. I'm sure baby number two will too. It will take a while to sort. Planning has gone in already, but I'm hoping within a year, I will have developed the site. I want to be with you mum. We've lost fifty years; I'm not going to allow any more to pass us by."

"What about your dad William. I don't want him to be left in Exeter alone. Joey and Evie are grown now. They have their own lives."

"Well, that's the other bit mum, I didn't say I was going to build one house. The plot is plenty bit enough for two. Dad wants to move too. Maybe I should put two Huff Houses on the site. I believe you're quite partial to a Huff House mum." We smiled at each other as I nudged him.

"What? Oh, William, what am I like. Well yes actually I do like Huff Houses. How is today evening happening. I will have you all here with me. I cannot quite believe all this."

"Fifty years mum. Enough is enough. We've found each other, now it's time to start building or rebuilding."

"Rebuilding?"

"Well dad is on his own mum. Moira was so lovely, but she's been passed for so long. Maybe it's time for dad to find happiness again. Maybe it's time for some rekindling of old feeling. This bench, on this beach eh Marjorie."

"William. Honestly. You and Hetty will get on like a house on fire."

We sat in silence. Our arms linked, our heads joined and watched as the sky turned from blue to navy. The gulls swooped and dived, and the grasses danced. The waves lapped gently against the sand and the story rested.

William was home.

I was home.

The End.

ABOUT THE AUTHOR

Raised in Birmingham, UK, Gráinne McGovern-Scott now lives in Chester with her husband John and dog Finn. She raised her two sons Samuel and Connor to love holidays and value the power of family and connection. Her love of the coast and her connection to it is now firmly instilled in them.

Gráinne wanted to write a novel that tackled the issue of loneliness and its many faces. As a child with an alcoholic father, Only the Lonely captures the pain and destruction alcoholism reigns down on a family and the loneliness it generates.

Printed in Dunstable, United Kingdom